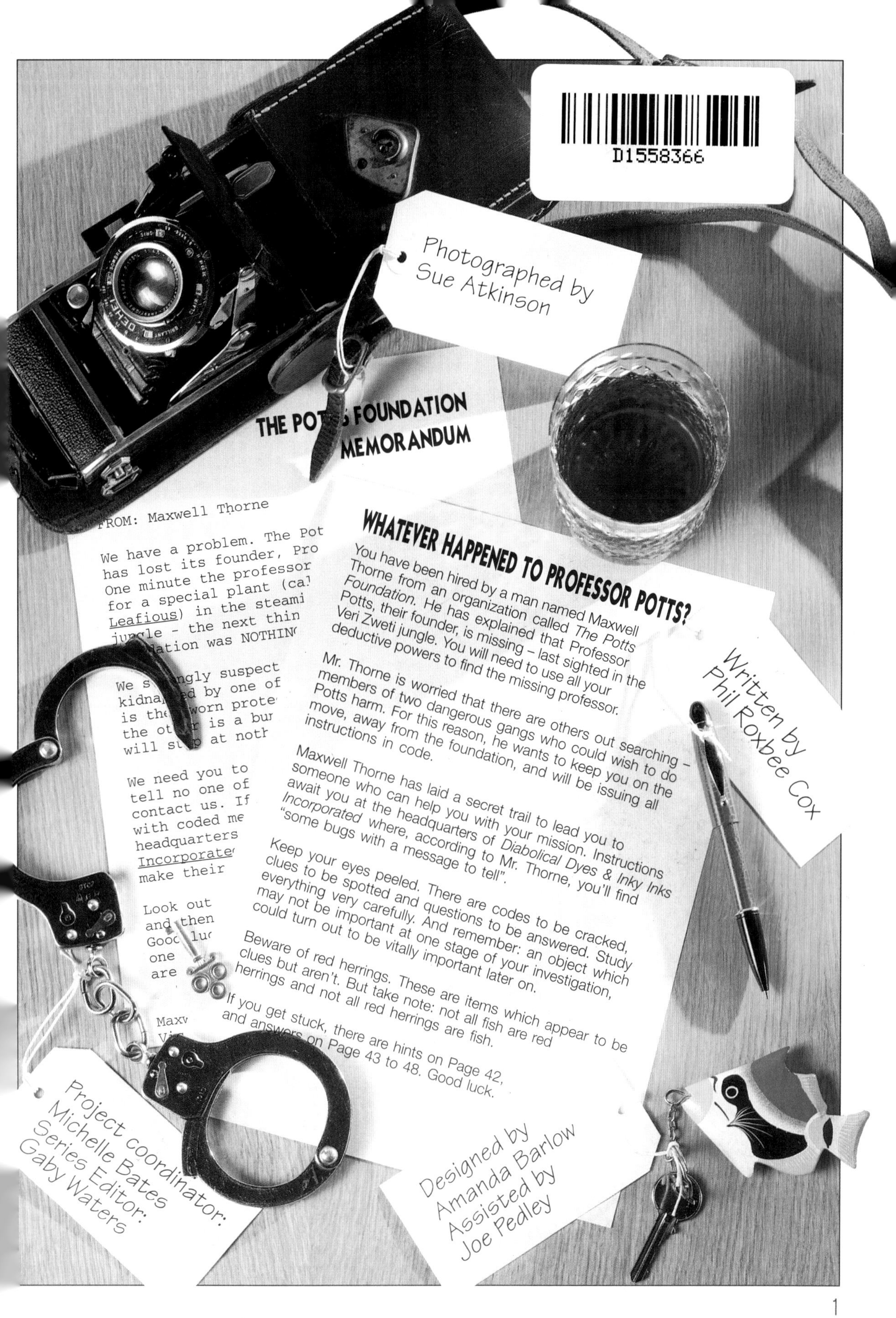
D1558366
Photographed by Sue Atkinson
THE POTTS FOUNDATION MEMORANDUM
FROM: Maxwell Thorne
We have a problem. The Pot
has lost its founder, Pro
One minute the professor
for a special plant (cal
Leafious) in the steami
jungle - the next thin
We strongly suspect
We need you to
tell no one of
contact us. If
with coded me
headquarters
Incorporated
make their
Look out
and then
Good luc
WHATEVER HAPPENED TO PROFESSOR POTTS?
You have been hired by a man named Maxwell Thorne from an organization called *The Potts Foundation*. He has explained that Professor Potts, their founder, is missing – last sighted in the Veri Zweti jungle. You will need to use all your deductive powers to find the missing professor.
Mr. Thorne is worried that there are others out searching – members of two dangerous gangs who could wish to do Potts harm. For this reason, he wants to keep you on the move, away from the foundation, and will be issuing all instructions in code.
Maxwell Thorne has laid a secret trail to lead you to someone who can help you with your mission. Instructions await you at the headquarters of *Diabolical Dyes & Inky Inks Incorporated* where, according to Mr. Thorne, you'll find "some bugs with a message to tell".
Keep your eyes peeled. There are codes to be cracked, clues to be spotted and questions to be answered. Study everything very carefully. And remember: an object which may not be important at one stage of your investigation, could turn out to be vitally important later on.
Beware of red herrings. These are items which appear to be clues but aren't. But take note: not all fish are red herrings and not all red herrings are fish.
If you get stuck, there are hints on Page 42, and answers on Page 43 to 48. Good luck.
Written by Phil Roxbee Cox
Project coordinator: Michelle Bates
Series Editor: Gaby Waters
Designed by Amanda Barlow
Assisted by Joe Pedley

4
8
6
3

THE MISSION BEGINS

Time: Thursday, 1:03pm
Place: 1st Floor, Headquarters
Diabolical Dyes & Inky Inks Incorporated

There's been a party here, but the building is now empty. In the corner of one room is a table. On the table is a dangerous-looking water pistol, and a group of insect cards. These must be the 'bugs with a message to tell'.

What does this message mean?

On
Your way
From under
The messiest desk
Go
In the building
Eat plenty
Of dates
The key
Take
The box
Home to a friend
5
1
7
2

THE SEARCH IS ON

Time: Thursday, 1:37pm
Place: The messiest desk, 120th Floor, Headquarters
Diabolical Dyes & Inky Inks Incorporated

The message mentioned a key under a box of dates. There's certainly plenty of other fruit around, but not one of them is a date or even a fig, which is the next best thing. There are boxes too – a flowery one, and one shaped like an Egyptian sarcophagus. Both are empty. There's nothing in them, on them, or under them. The clock has stopped, but there's no key under it either. A waste of time?

Where is the key hidden?

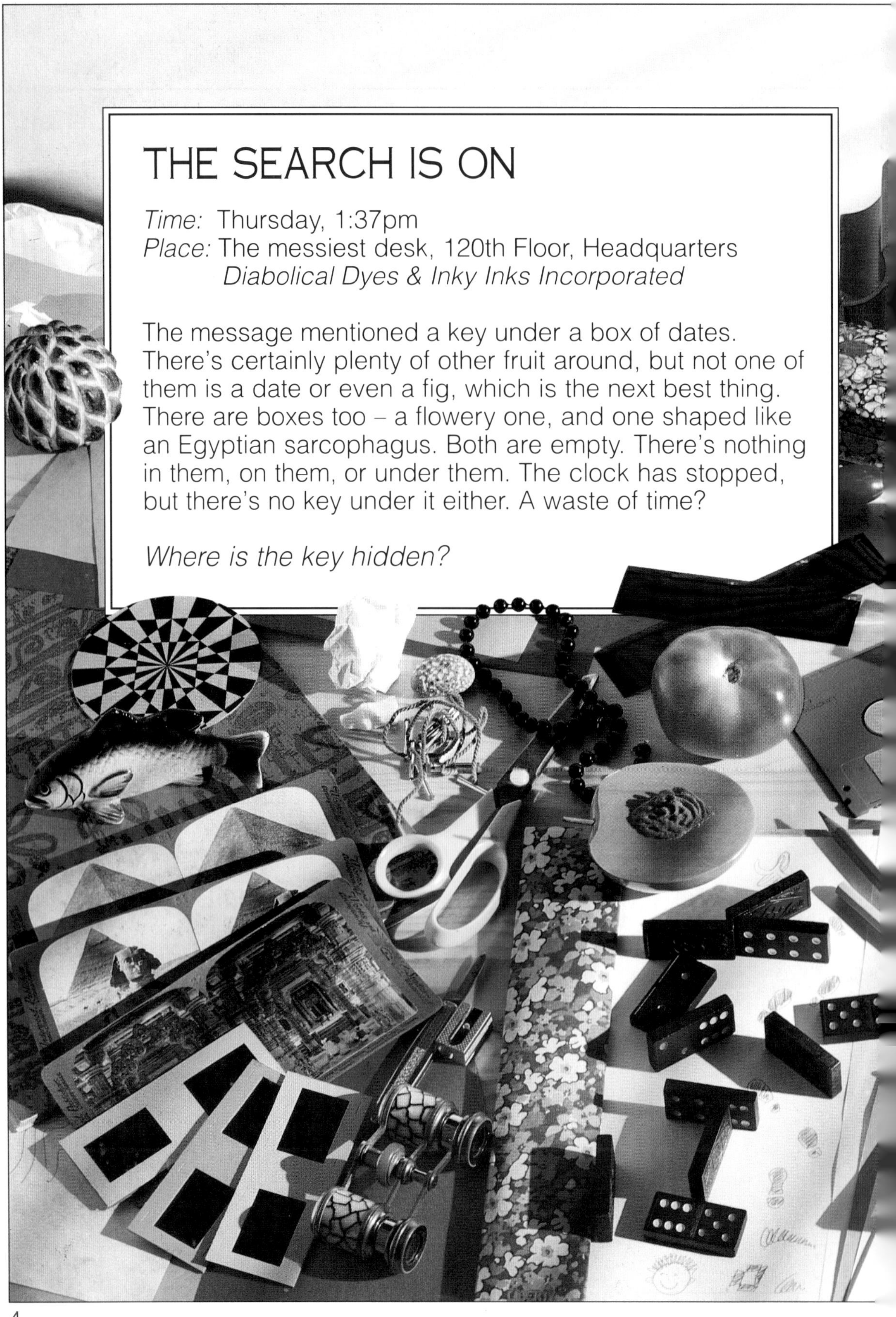

Diabolical
Dyes & Inky
Inks Inc.
Ext: 482
1 1 SEP

EXPENSES
INSTR TIONS

GP22657
141
Box 33
3rd National
Bank
Thrift Street

DEEP IN THE VAULT

Time: Thursday, 2:18pm
Place: Third National Bank, Uptown

The key opens a safety deposit box at the address shown on the tag. Inside the box is a bundle of money in an envelope marked **EXPENSES**, a few oddments, some coded instructions, and a gallery of torn up photographs.

PhReOrFeEiSsSaOcRaPrOkTeTySbPeRlOoFnEgSiSnOgRtPoOt ThTeSoPnReOpFeErSsSoOnRpPhOoTtToSgPrRaOpFhEeSdSw OiRtPhOoTuTtSaPnRaOnFiEmSaSlOvRiPsOiTtTtShPeRpOeFr EsSoSnOaRtPoOnTcTeS

What do these instructions say?

DEAD END!

Time: Thursday, 3:27pm
Place: Dr. Karl Otta's *Plant Import Export Company*, Downtown

On the back of the bearded man's photo is the name Dr. Karl Otta and an address: Plant Import Export Company, 12a Flash St., Downtown. This is a grand title for a stuffy little office above a sock factory. The room is buzzing with bugs but Dr. Karl Otta doesn't seem to mind. He's very dead. Probably murdered.

If he was murdered, how recently could it have happened?

THE FISH HEADS

THE SEARCH FOR CLUES

Time: Thursday, 3:57pm
Place Dr. Karl Otta's car. Parking Lot.
Rear of *Plant Import Export Company*

The car key from the safety deposit box unlocks Karl Otta's old car. There is a pile of odds and ends on the passenger seat. A golf ball . . . a bottle of poison . . . a starting pistol . . . a crystal ball . . . There's something familiar here. A symbol? A sign?

What is it?

THE SNAKE BITE CLUB
It's party time again!
Why not slither your way down to AL'S for a night to remember.
Everyone welcome Friday September 8th
Not only snakes have scales. Pianos do too. Learn to play the easy way. Ask at the bar for details.
Plan to travel far?
Then why not rent a car
TOOTS CAR RENTAL ha
car for you. Near or fa
rent a TOOTS CAR.
Phone:
555-000-555-000
ALL HATS AND COATS TO BE CHECKED IN ON ARRIVAL. DON'T LOSE YOUR TICKET.
NO TICKET, NO COAT.
451
GP22657

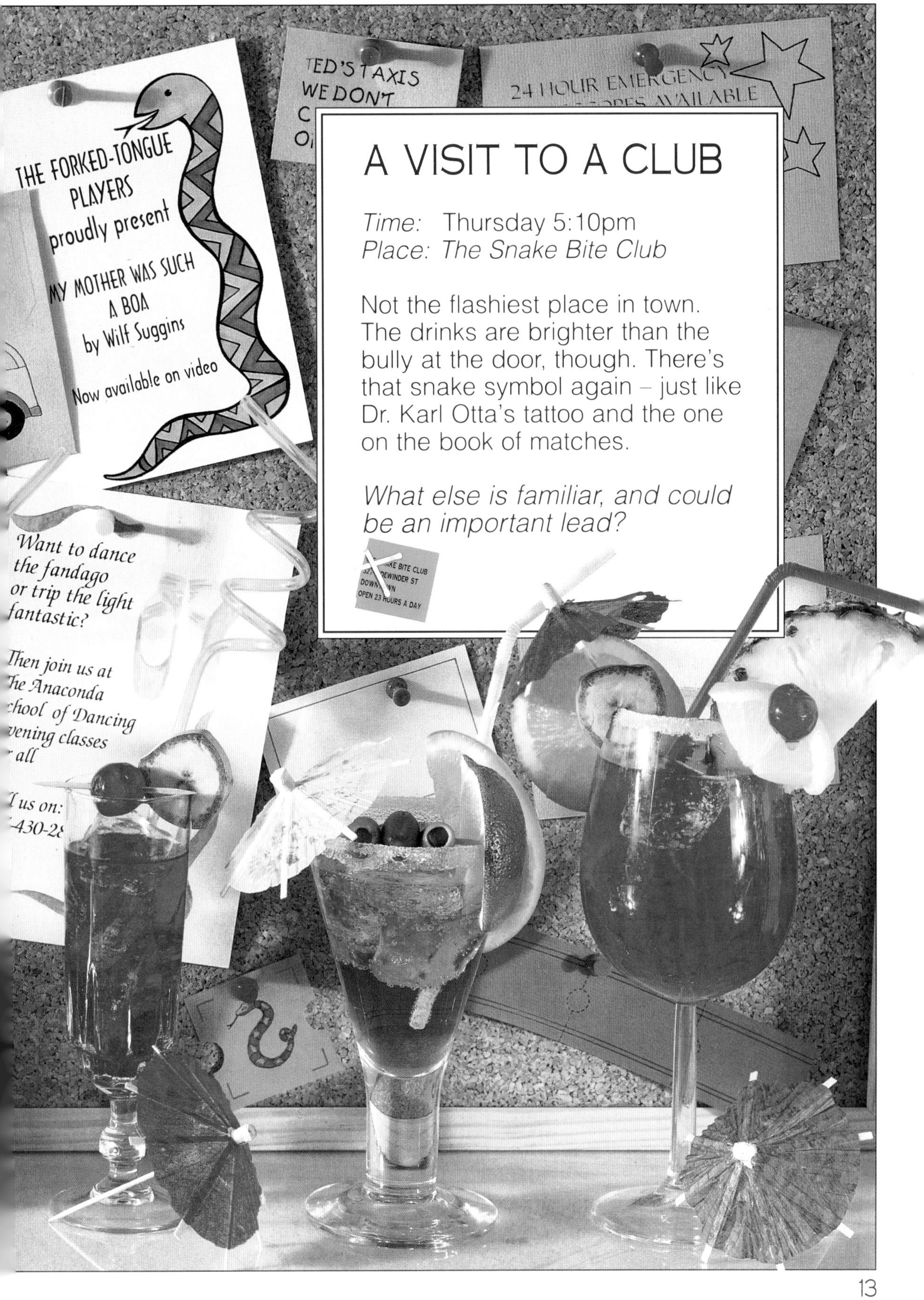
THE FORKED-TONGUE PLAYERS
proudly present
MY MOTHER WAS SUCH A BOA
by Wilf Suggins
Now available on video
TED'S TAXIS
WE DON'T
24 HOUR EMERGENCY
Want to dance
the fandago
or trip the light
fantastic?
OPEN 23 HOURS A DAY

A VISIT TO A CLUB

Time: Thursday 5:10pm
Place: The Snake Bite Club

Not the flashiest place in town. The drinks are brighter than the bully at the door, though. There's that snake symbol again – just like Dr. Karl Otta's tattoo and the one on the book of matches.

What else is familiar, and could be an important lead?

DEAD MAN'S CLOTHES

Time: Thursday, 5:33pm
Place: A doorway. Across the street from the *Snake Bite Club*

In return for the pink ticket from the safety deposit box, comes a coat with the name *K. OTTA* sewn onto the lining, with a message: *IF FOUND, PLEASE RETURN TO OWNER'S OFFICE*. The coat was heavy. No wonder. There was masses of stuff in the pockets. The contents now lie in a doorway, lighted by a street lamp. Most of it looks like garbage. Most of it *is* garbage, and the money is bad news.

Why?

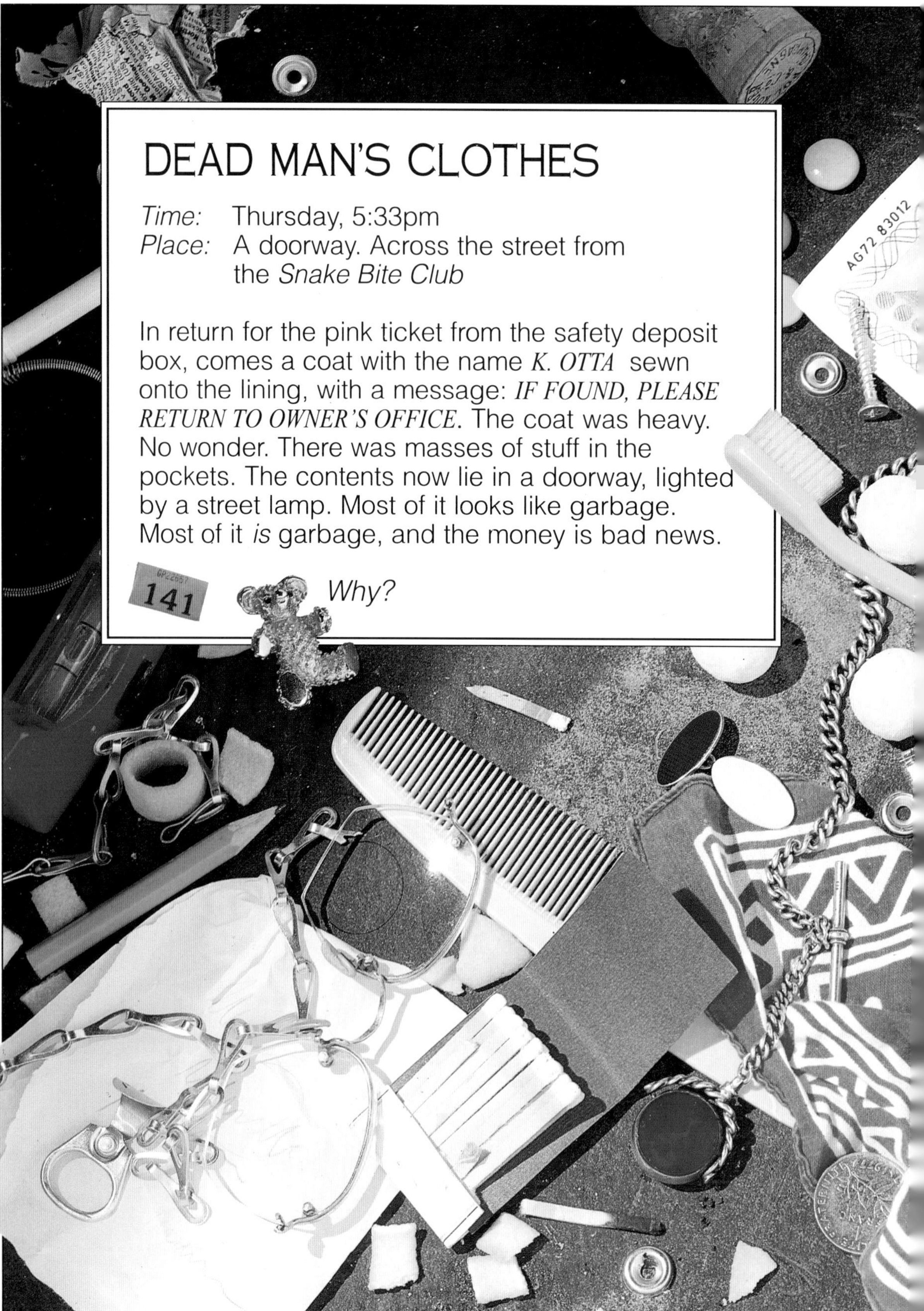
141
AG72 83012

RANSACKED!

Time: Thursday, 5:45pm
Place: Dr. Karl Otta's *Plant Import and Export Company*
Returning coat to (dead) owner

Someone else has paid Dr. Karl Otta's office a visit. It could be the cleaners because the body has certainly been cleared away . . . but that's unlikely. The rest of the place is such a mess and the bugs haven't been dusted. The visitor has taken more than just the body, and dropped something too.

What is missing, and what's new?

This is Potts's journal,
a map of Sprunga Leeki,
and a model of a village.
My secret sign
A friendly
bug
My whereabouts:
Some Quiz Us About
Recent Expedition And
They Have Reservations,
Expecting Excitement!

PLANS MAPPED OUT

Time: Friday, 9:11am
Place: Fairly Central Park,
after a restless night

A large package has arrived. Inside is a book that was on the table at *Diabolical Dyes & Inky Inks Incorporated*. It's Professor Potts's journal. There's also a model village and a map. And a coded clue to the professor's last-known location.

Where, on the map, was Potts?

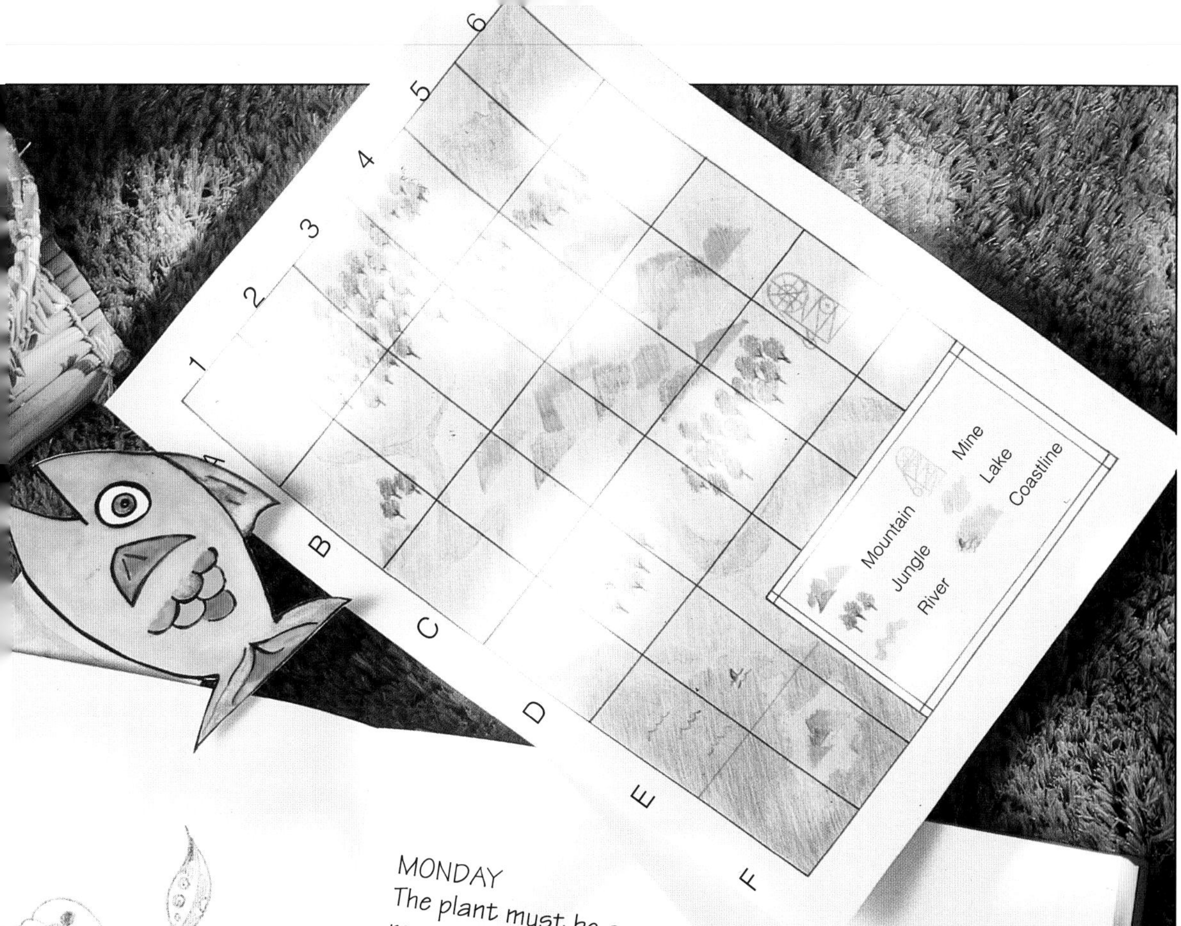
1
2
3
4
5
6
B
C
D
E
F
Mountain
Jungle
River
Mine
Lake
Coastline

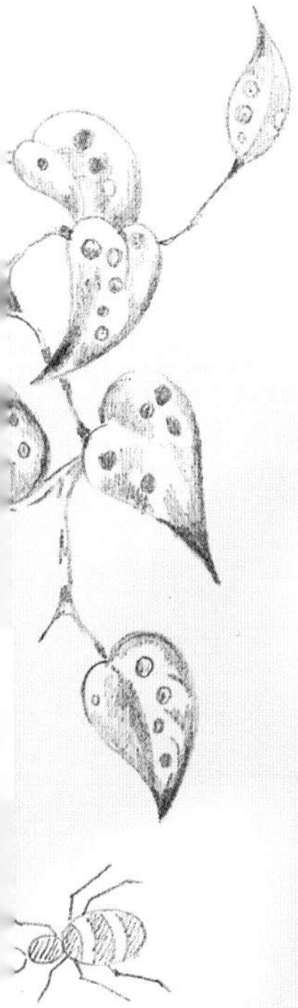

MONDAY

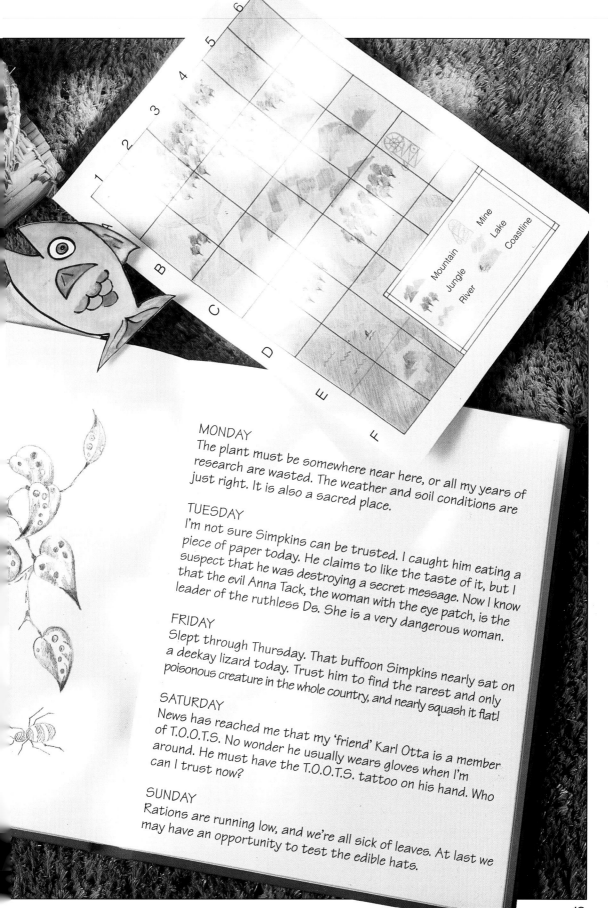

The plant must be somewhere near here, or all my years of research are wasted. The weather and soil conditions are just right. It is also a sacred place.

TUESDAY

I'm not sure Simpkins can be trusted. I caught him eating a piece of paper today. He claims to like the taste of it, but I suspect that he was destroying a secret message. Now I know that the evil Anna Tack, the woman with the eye patch, is the leader of the ruthless Ds. She is a very dangerous woman.

FRIDAY

Slept through Thursday. That buffoon Simpkins nearly sat on a deekay lizard today. Trust him to find the rarest and only poisonous creature in the whole country, and nearly squash it flat!

SATURDAY

News has reached me that my 'friend' Karl Otta is a member of T.O.O.T.S. No wonder he usually wears gloves when I'm around. He must have the T.O.O.T.S. tattoo on his hand. Who can I trust now?

SUNDAY

Rations are running low, and we're all sick of leaves. At last we may have an opportunity to test the edible hats.

UP IN THE AIR

Time: Friday, 12:35pm
Place: Seat D5. *Flight 01424* to Sprunga Leeki on the way to finding Potts's last known location

The person in seat D6 is laying cards onto a briefcase on her lap. She's the woman with the feather boa in one of the photographs from the safety deposit box. What's her game? Not just cards, that's for sure. An item on her briefcase suggests it is something far deadlier . . .

What is it?

DOWN TO EARTH

Time: Friday 3:06pm local time
Place: Runway,
Sprunga Leeki Airport

It's hot. The temperature is somewhere between sweltering and unbearable. A fellow passenger drops his case on the runway. Things tumble and roll everywhere. From the look of his dice, he's not the sort of person to leave anything to chance. He also seems to have something fishy in more ways than one.

What is it?

NARODOWY
500

HOTEL
ELISABETTA
RAPALLO

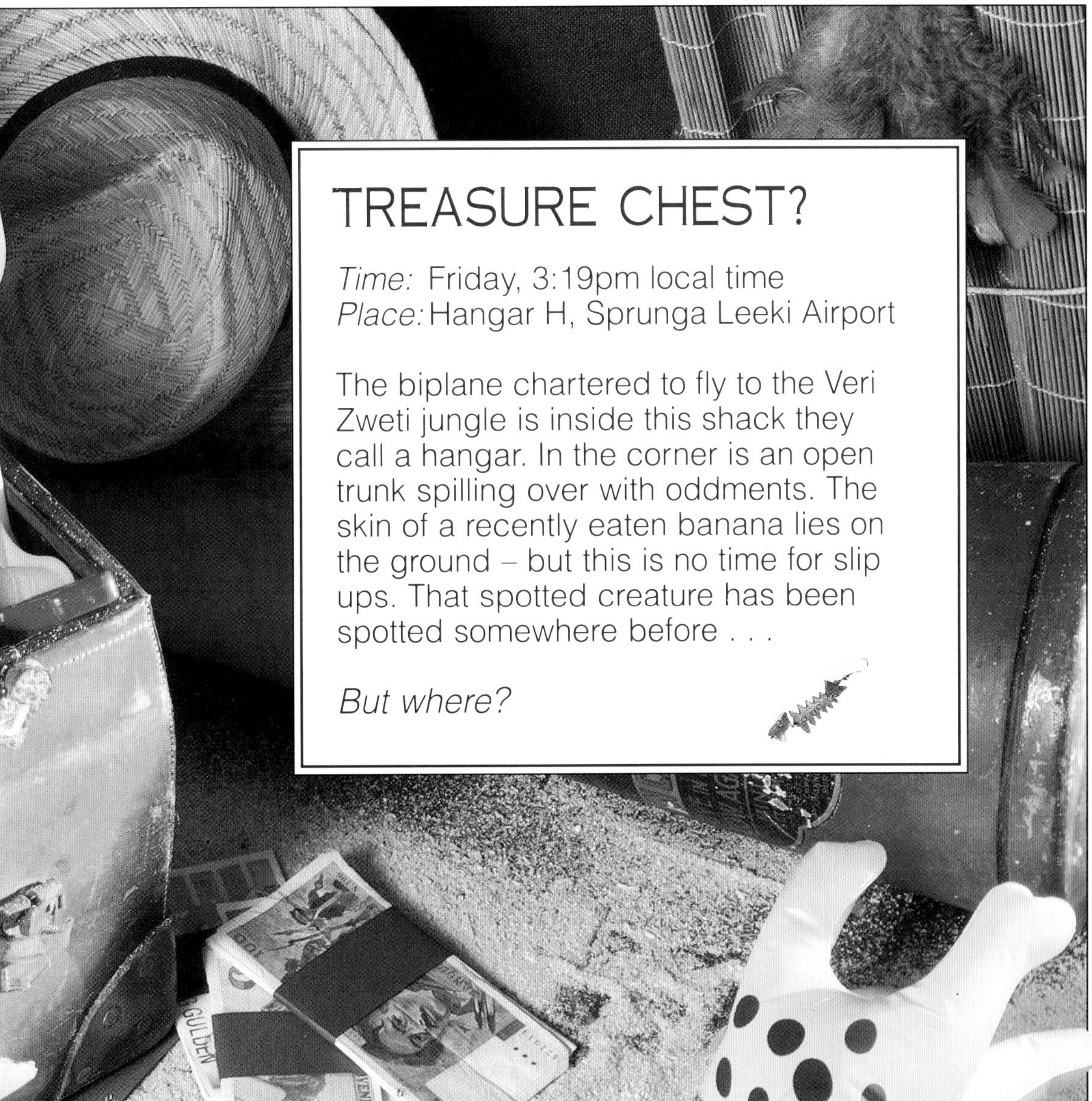
GULDEN

TREASURE CHEST?

Time: Friday, 3:19pm local time
Place: Hangar H, Sprunga Leeki Airport

The biplane chartered to fly to the Veri Zweti jungle is inside this shack they call a hangar. In the corner is an open trunk spilling over with oddments. The skin of a recently eaten banana lies on the ground – but this is no time for slip ups. That spotted creature has been spotted somewhere before . . .

But where?

TO THE JUNGLE!

Time: Friday, 5:12pm local time
Place: Veri Zweti jungle, at location recorded in Potts's journal

The biplane has landed in a clearing. Through the trees is a rock just waiting to be found and, beyond that, an ancient, ruined temple covered in creepy creepers. This must be the 'sacred place' that the professor wrote about in the journal. Potts has left behind a very simple message.

What is it?

HOT ON THE TRAIL

Time: Friday, 5:47pm local time
Place: Veri Zweti jungle, in the ruined temple at the end of the arrow trail

Professor Potts's trail of arrows ends by a wall, and with a message in a water bottle. At first glance, the message makes about as much sense as eating soup with a fork.

What does it say?

My life is in great danger now that I have found the special plant. It only grows inside the ruins of this great temple and is of interest to two powerful organizations. One, The Order Of The Serpent, has kept this location and the plant's amazing powers a secret for a thousand years. Each member has a special snake tattoo.
The other organization has evil aims. Called the Dominants, its members plan to use some of the special plant's powers as a mind control drug. They want to turn the population into mindless slaves. They each wear the ring of the Evil Eye.
Both groups want to stop my work. I'll only be safe when the report on my discoveries here are published. It includes the formula to an antidote to the mind control drug. Once that is done, it will be too late for them to try to silence me. Until then, I shall go into hiding. So, whoever is reading this, please understand that I don't want to be found. Go home.

SNAKE TROUBLE!

Time: Friday, 7:23 local time
Place: Lost somewhere in the Veri Zweti jungle, searching for the biplane

Nightfall. There's a light up ahead, but it's not coming from the biplane. There's a candle and a fruit feast for snake lovers. Toy snakes are everywhere . . . and, in among them, one that's very much alive and slithering from a box of half-eaten hats.

Is the snake dangerous?

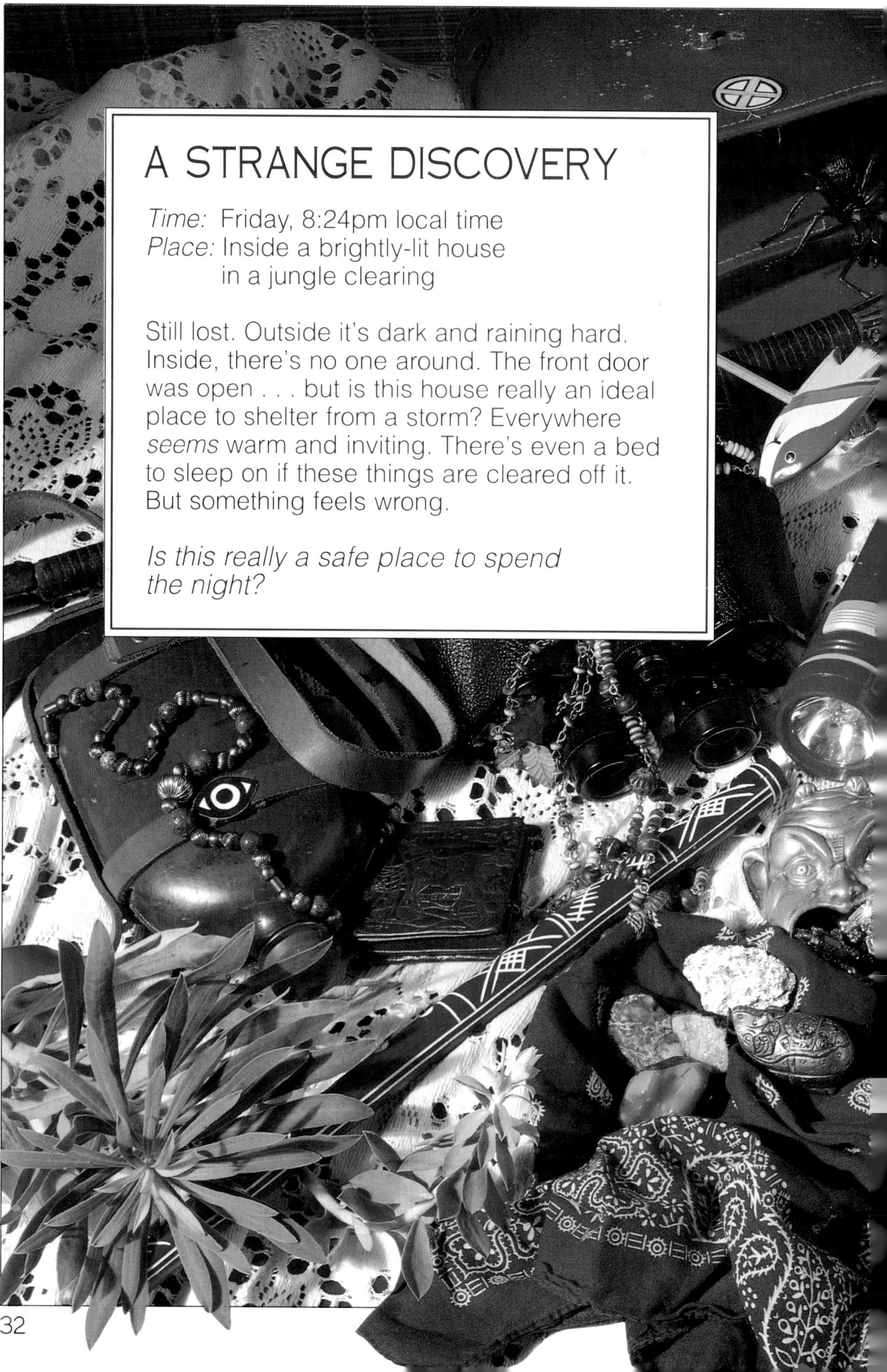

A STRANGE DISCOVERY

Time: Friday, 8:24pm local time
Place: Inside a brightly-lit house in a jungle clearing

Still lost. Outside it's dark and raining hard. Inside, there's no one around. The front door was open . . . but is this house really an ideal place to shelter from a storm? Everywhere *seems* warm and inviting. There's even a bed to sleep on if these things are cleared off it. But something feels wrong.

Is this really a safe place to spend the night?

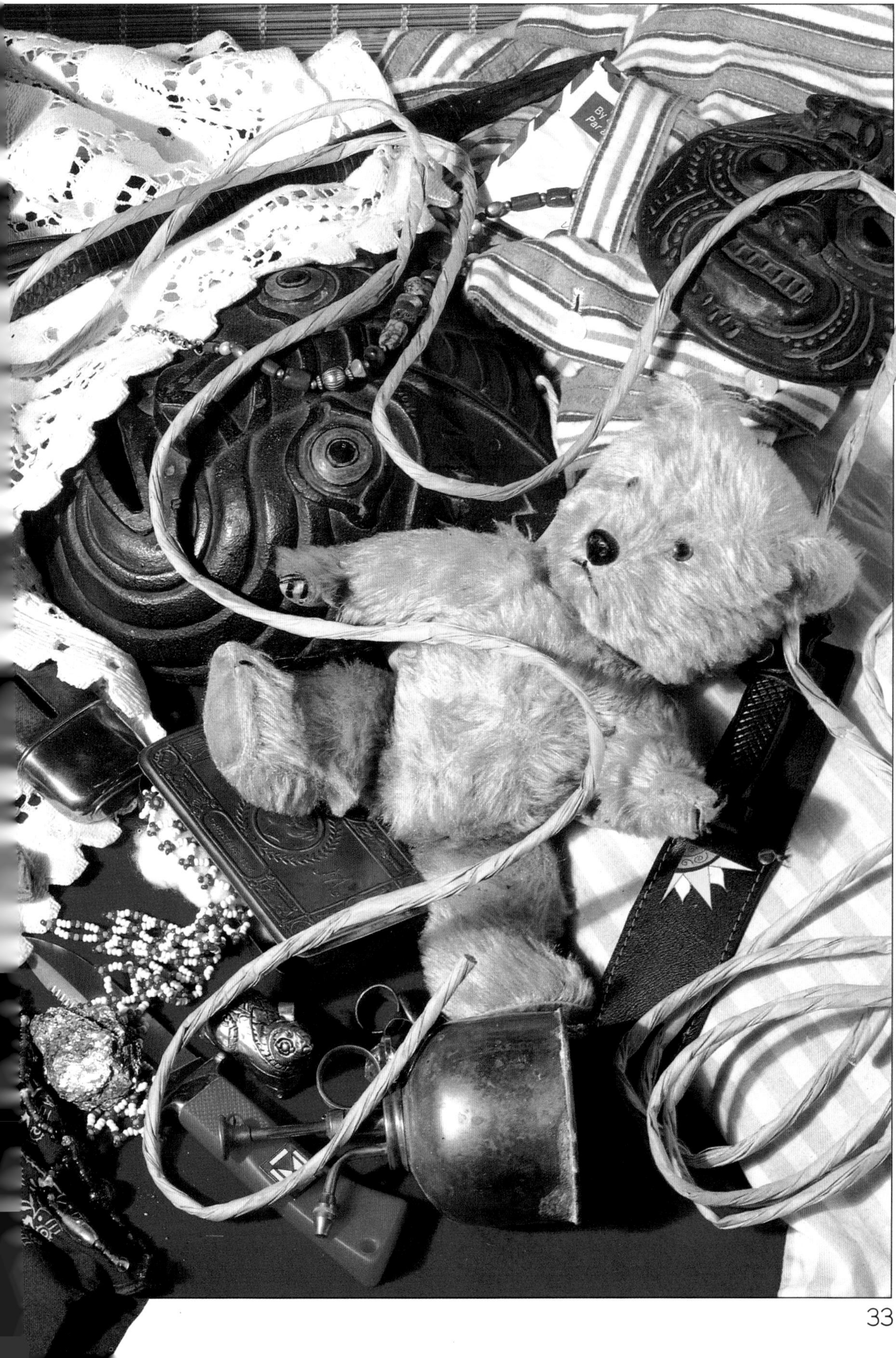

DANGER SIGNS

Time: Saturday, 6.34am local time
Place: On the veranda of the house in the jungle. The biplane is now visible in the distance

In the glow of the rising sun, golden objects glint and sparkle on a wicker chair. The bright yellow water pistol is filled with mosquito repellent. The notebook is full of blank pages. Mysterious messages written in invisible ink, perhaps? There's an object here that was last seen in the hands of someone very dangerous . . . It's time to leave in a hurry.

Which object means danger, and why?

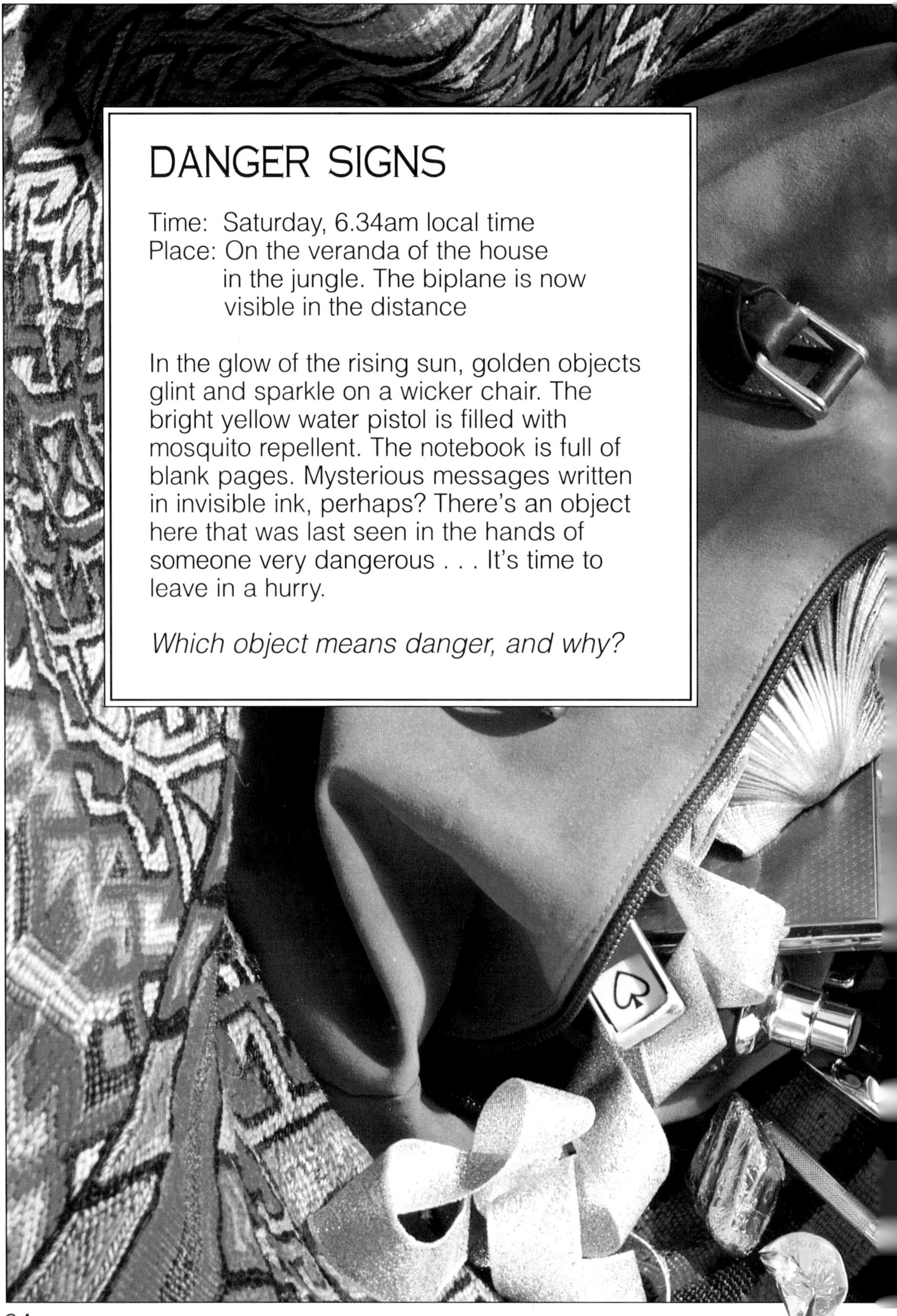

Diabolical
Dyes & Inky
Inks Inc.
Ext: 482
MON
11
SEP

BACK TO THE BEGINNING

Time: Sunday, 9.54am
Place: Messiest desk, 120th Floor, Head Office
Diabolical Dyes & Inky Inks Incorporated

Back on familiar territory after a wasted journey and a good night's sleep. Is Professor Potts still in hiding as the coded message suggested? Not allowed to contact the *Potts Foundation*. Perhaps *Diabolical Dyes & Inky Inks Incorporated* holds some more clues. Hence a second visit. Looking in the mirror, the messiest desk looks different – and not just because it's a mirror image.

What items are missing?

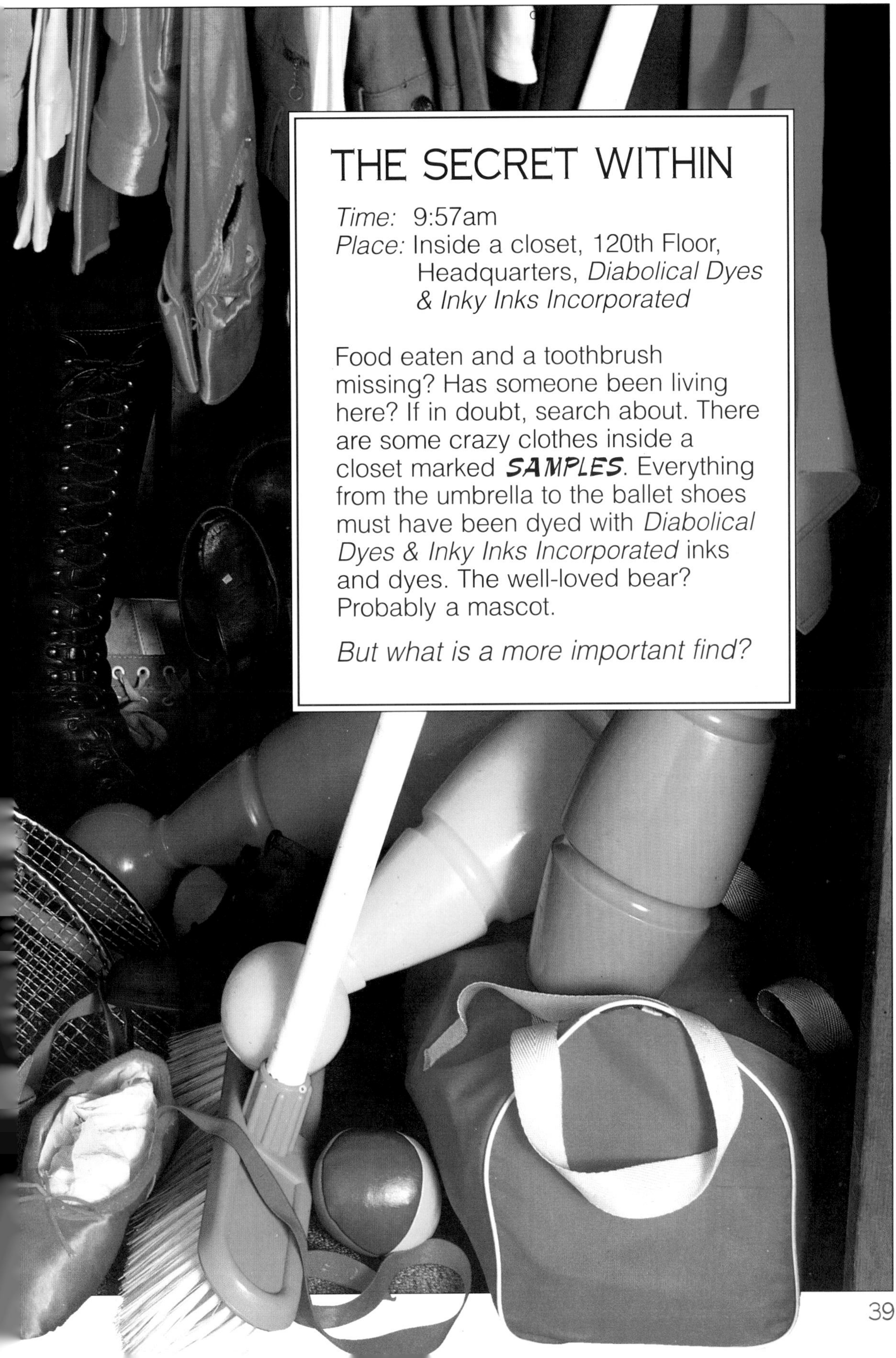

THE SECRET WITHIN

Time: 9:57am
Place: Inside a closet, 120th Floor, Headquarters, *Diabolical Dyes & Inky Inks Incorporated*

Food eaten and a toothbrush missing? Has someone been living here? If in doubt, search about. There are some crazy clothes inside a closet marked **SAMPLES**. Everything from the umbrella to the ballet shoes must have been dyed with *Diabolical Dyes & Inky Inks Incorporated* inks and dyes. The well-loved bear? Probably a mascot.

But what is a more important find?

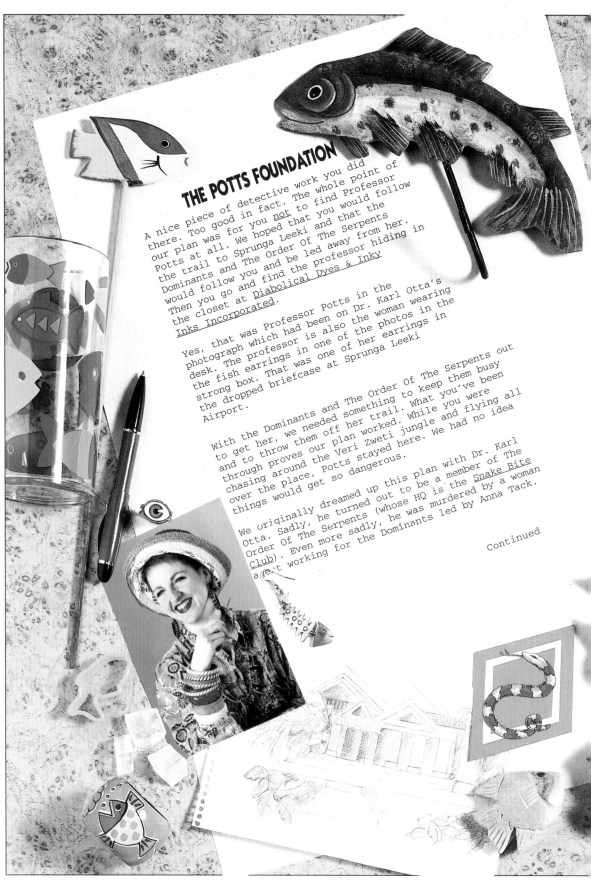

THE POTTS FOUNDATION

A nice piece of detective work you did there. Too good in fact. The whole point of our plan was for you not to find Professor Potts at all. We hoped that you would follow the trail to Sprunga Leeki and that the Dominants and The Order Of The Serpents would follow you and be led away from her. Then you go and find the professor hiding in the closet at Diabolical Dyes & Inky Inks Incorporated.

Yes, that was Professor Potts in the photograph which had been on Dr. Karl Otta's desk. The professor is also the woman wearing the fish earrings in one of the photos in the strong box. That was one of her earrings in the dropped briefcase at Sprunga Leeki Airport.

With the Dominants and The Order Of The Serpents out to get her, we needed something to keep them busy and to throw them off her trail. What you've been through proves our plan worked. While you were chasing around the Veri Zweti jungle and flying all over the place, Potts stayed here. We had no idea things would get so dangerous.

We originally dreamed up this plan with Dr. Karl Otta. Sadly, he turned out to be a member of The Order Of The Serpents (whose HQ is the Snake Bite Club). Even more sadly, he was murdered by a woman agent working for the Dominants led by Anna Tack.

Continued

Must remember to order some more Potts Foundation letterheaded paper

The man who dropped his case was a member of the T.O.O.T.S. keeping an eye on you in the hope of finding the professor. (He must have found one of her fish earrings when on the trail.)

Now that her research has been published Professor Potts is free to live a normal again. Congratulations on all your hard wo

Next week, the professor flies to Mount Thunder in search of the Lost Lettuce of Phoenix Rock. Until then, she plans to do some weeding in the garden.

Maxwell Thorne

Maxwell Thorne
Vice-President

P.S. Sorry about the fake money we paid you for expenses. It came from Dr. Karl Otta before we realized that he was mixed up with the gangs.

HELPFUL HINTS

PAGES 2 & 3
Try matching the large bugs to the smaller ones.

PAGES 4 & 5
Dates aren't just a sort of fruit.

PAGES 6 & 7
Try removing the capital letters.

PAGES 8 & 9
Things that tell the time hold the vital clues.

PAGES 10 & 11
Look back at Dr. Karl Otta – or what we can see of him.

PAGES 12 & 13
There are more than just notices on the noticeboard.

PAGES 14 & 15
Where else have you seen similar money?

PAGES 16 & 17
Look back to pages 8 & 9.

PAGES 18 & 19
Look at the first letter of each word in the coded clue. This should help you to use the map!

PAGES 20 & 21
Can you see anything familiar? Look back to pages 8 & 9.

PAGES 22 & 23
"Fishy in more ways than one" is important here. The object was last seen in a photograph of someone.

PAGES 24 & 25
You've only seen a picture of it before now.

PAGES 26 & 27
Look back to Professor Potts's journal on pages 18 &19.

PAGES 28 & 29
A mirror might help you.

PAGES 30 & 31
It will help if you look back to what Potts said on page 19 about animals in the Veri Zweti jungle.

PAGES 32 & 33
Study the symbols carefully.

PAGES 34 & 35
You'll need a clue from the photos in the safety deposit box on pages 6 & 7 and some information from Potts's journal on pages 18 & 19.

PAGES 36 & 37
The answers are a mouthful.

PAGES 38 & 39
Someone has put her foot in it.

ANSWERS

PAGES 2 & 3

The card covered in small bugs and a meaningless message is, in fact, the key to the real message. Match the bugs on the numbered cards against the bugs on the key card. Write down the words to the right of the matching bugs, and then read them in the order of the numbered cards 1 to 8. The message reads:
Take the key from under the box of dates on the messiest desk in the building.

PAGES 4 & 5

The word *dates* in the message is not referring to dates as in fruit. It is referring to dates as in the day and the month. The key is under the box-shaped calendar.

MON
1
1
SEP

PAGES 6 & 7

The capital letters spell out the name *PROFESSOR POTTS* over and over again. Remove them and you will be left with a message. Decoded and with punctuation added it reads:
Here is a car key belonging to the one person photographed without an animal. Visit the person at once.

PAGES 8 & 9

The clock on the desk reads the correct time (3:27). Dr. Karl Otta's broken watch, however, reads 1:19. It is likely that the doctor's watch was broken when he was attacked. This means that he could have been attacked just over two hours ago.

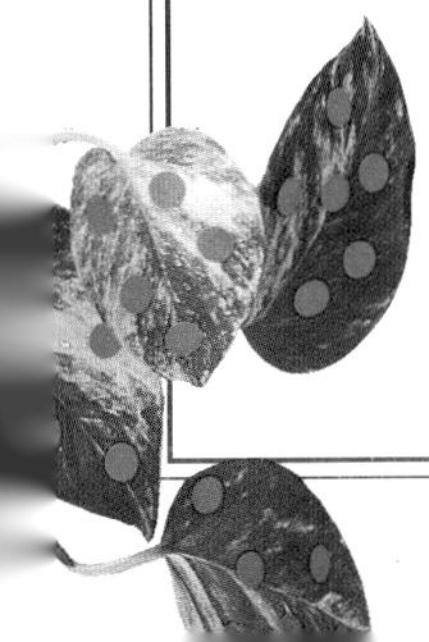

PAGES 10 & 11

The snake symbol on the green book of matches is similar to the tiny snake tattoo on Dr. Karl Otta's hand on pages 9 & 10.

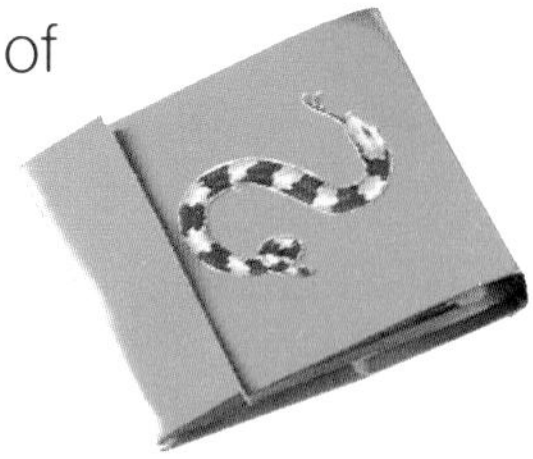

PAGES 12 & 13

Look at the notice that reads: **ALL HATS AND COATS TO BE CHECKED IN ON ARRIVAL. DON'T LOSE YOUR TICKET. NO TICKET, NO COAT.** Next to it is a pink ticket that is similar to the pink ticket (Number 141) from the safety deposit box.

GP22657
451

GP22657
141

PAGES 14 & 15

All serial numbers on banknotes and bills are different. The number on this Sprunga Leeki dollar bill, however, matches the number on the top bill in the envelope marked **EXPENSES** on pages 6 & 7. This means that either some, or all, of this money is fake. Worthless.

PAGES 16 & 17

The framed photo of the woman is missing. In its place is an empty frame and a lipstick that wasn't there before.

PAGES 18 & 19

The first letter from each word under the journal entry: "My *whereabouts*" spells (with the correct spacing) SQUARE A THREE. Square A3 in the map is on the middle of a jungle area. This was Potts's last location.

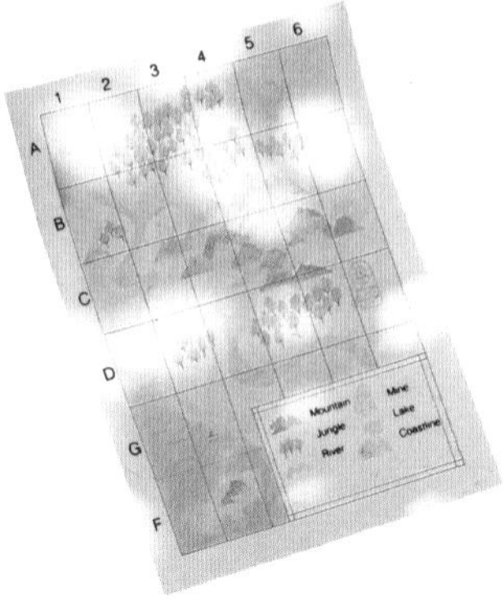
1
2
3
4
5
6
A
B
C
D
G
F

PAGES 20 & 21

Even though it is showing a different time, that is definitely Dr. Karl Otta's broken watch in the top left-hand corner of the case. The last time you saw it, it was on the dead man's wrist.

PAGES 22 & 23

There is a silver fish earring in the briefcase. It matches those worn by a woman in one of the torn-up photographs in the vault of the Third National Bank on pages 6 & 7.

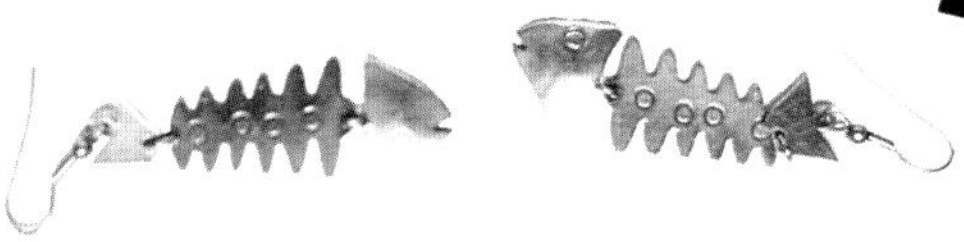

PAGES 24 & 25

The spotted creature appears with the woman in a photograph. It's the one on Dr. Karl Otta's desk at his *Plant Import Export Company* on pages 8 & 9.

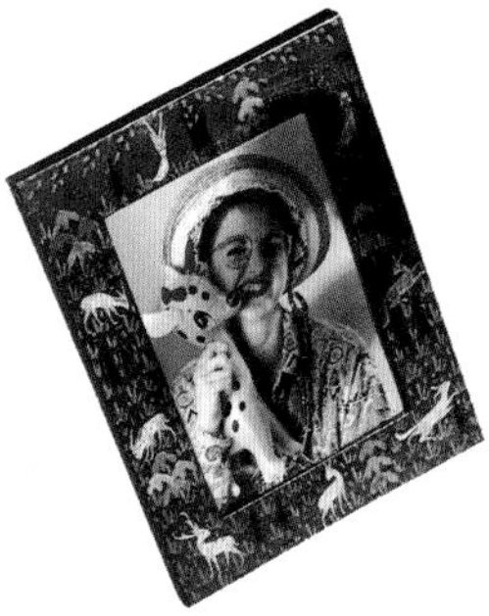

PAGES 26 & 27

Among the patterns drawn on the rock is the symbol  and an arrow. The same symbol appears on pages 18 & 19. It is next to a note saying "My *secret sign*", in the professor's journal. The message on the rock, therefore, must be simply to follow the arrow.

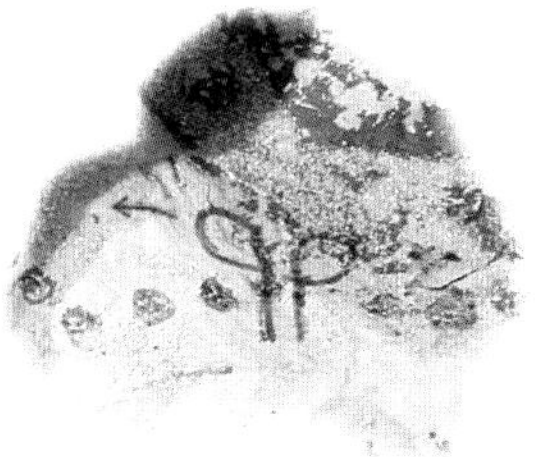

PAGES 28 & 29

The message is in mirror writing. Simply turn the book upside down and hold it in front of a mirror to read it. There's some very important information in this message, so read it carefully.

My life is in great danger now that I have found the special plant. It only grows inside the ruins of this great temple and is of interest to two powerful organizations. One, The Order of The Serpent, has kept this location and the plant's amazing powers a secret for a thousand years. Each member has a special snake tattoo.

The other organization has evil aims. Called the Dominants, its members plan to use some of the special plant's powers as a mind control drug. They want to turn the population into mindless slaves. They each wear the ring of the Evil Eye.

Both groups want to stop my work. I'll only be safe when the report on my discoveries here are published. It includes the formula to an antidote to the mind control drug. Once that is done, it will be too late for them to try to silence me. Until then, I shall go into hiding. So, whoever is reading this, please understand that I don't want to be found. Go home.

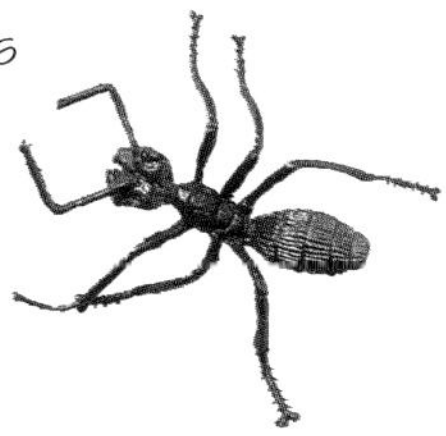

POTTS

PAGES 30 & 31

In Friday's entry in the journal on pages 18 & 19, Professor Potts describes the deekay lizard as *"the only poisonous creature in the whole country..."*. This would suggest that the snake here is harmless ... Then again, it might have been flown in from abroad!

PAGES 32 & 33

The eye symbol on the large water bottle matches an eye symbol on a piece of crumpled paper. The paper is on pages 20 & 21 – on a woman's briefcase on-board *Flight 01424* to Sprunga Leeki.
The woman on the plane is wearing an eye ring. In Potts's message left in the ruins of the temple on pages 28 & 29, you are told that members of the Dominants wear "*the ring of the* Evil Eye". This means that the woman must be a member of the dangerous Dominants gang – and connects this house in the jungle to the gang.
Beware!

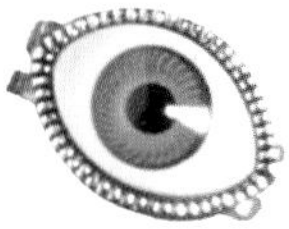

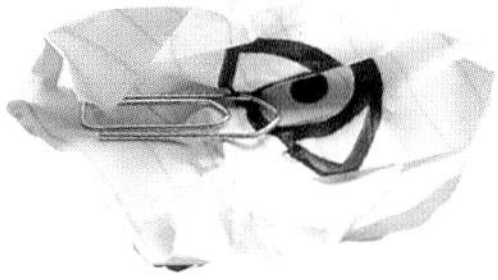

PAGES 34 & 35

You have seen this giant pocket watch somewhere before. It appeared in a photograph from the safety deposit box on pages 6 & 7. It was held by a woman wearing an eye patch. In the journal on pages 18 & 19, Potts has written that the "*evil Anna Tack, the woman with the eye patch, is the leader of the ruthless Ds. She is a very dangerous woman.*"
From the information on 28 & 29, it is obvious that by writing Ds, the professor means the Dominants. The giant pocket watch must belong to Anna Tack herself.

PAGES 36 & 37

Cherries and cakes have been eaten, and the toothbrush is missing from the pen holder by the telephone. Perhaps the person who ate the food then brushed his, or her, teeth?

PAGES 38 & 39

Look closely and you'll see that there are trouser legs coming out of the top of those boots. Someone is hiding in the **SAMPLES** closet!

DID YOU KNOW?

There is at least one fish on every double page – from fish-shaped keyrings to a fish bookmark.

On pages 40 & 41, you'll find most of the fish that appear elsewhere in the book. But not all. Some fish are missing and some are new. See if you can tell which are which.

DID YOU SPOT?

Dr. Karl Otta wasn't the only one with a snake tattoo. A man in one of the safety deposit box photographs, on pages 6 & 7, had one on his cheek as well.

There were edible hats in the box on pages 30 & 31. Professor Potts mentioned them in the journal on pages 18 & 19.

On pages 4 & 5, the clock on the messiest desk at the headquarters of *Diabolical Dyes & Inky Inks Incorporated* had stopped. On pages 36 & 37, however, it is showing a different time of day . . . but still the wrong one.

The car rental company advertised on the Snake Bite Club noticeboard on pages 12 & 13 is called T.O.O.T.S Car Rental. Did you realize that T.O.O.T.S stood for The Order Of The Serpent?

In the photograph on pages 40 & 41, Professor Potts was wearing some of the bracelets from the trunk on pages 24 & 25.

The crystals in the tin on pages 26 & 27, appeared next to the photograph of Potts on pages 40 & 41. They are made from the special plant that caused all the trouble.

The tiny snakes on pages 30 & 31 might not be plastic after all. One of them appears to be eating some fruit.

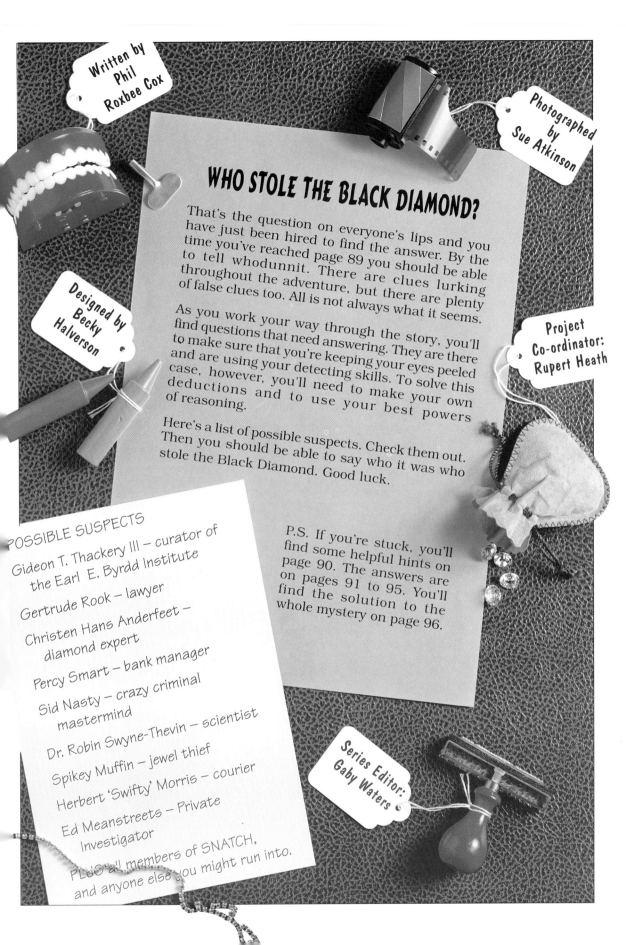

Written by Phil Roxbee Cox

Photographed by Sue Atkinson

Designed by Becky Halverson

Project Co-ordinator: Rupert Heath

Series Editor: Gaby Waters

WHO STOLE THE BLACK DIAMOND?

That's the question on everyone's lips and you have just been hired to find the answer. By the time you've reached page 89 you should be able to tell whodunnit. There are clues lurking throughout the adventure, but there are plenty of false clues too. All is not always what it seems.

As you work your way through the story, you'll find questions that need answering. They are there to make sure that you're keeping your eyes peeled and are using your detecting skills. To solve this case, however, you'll need to make your own deductions and to use your best powers of reasoning.

Here's a list of possible suspects. Check them out. Then you should be able to say who it was who stole the Black Diamond. Good luck.

POSSIBLE SUSPECTS

Gideon T. Thackery III – curator of the Earl E. Byrdd Institute

Gertrude Rook – lawyer

Christen Hans Anderfeet – diamond expert

Percy Smart – bank manager

Sid Nasty – crazy criminal mastermind

Dr. Robin Swyne-Thevin – scientist

Spikey Muffin – jewel thief

Herbert 'Swifty' Morris – courier

Ed Meanstreets – Private Investigator

PLUS all members of SNATCH, and anyone else you might run into.

P.S. If you're stuck, you'll find some helpful hints on page 90. The answers are on pages 91 to 95. You'll find the solution to the whole mystery on page 96.

READ ALL ABOUT IT

Time: Thursday, 8:47pm
Place: Brenda's Breakfast Bar

Your orange juice may be murky, but your mission is clear. The *Black Diamond* has been stolen and you've been hired to find it. The newspaper clippings should give you some useful information. The iced doughnut should give you some energy.

How much is the Black Diamond worth?
Where was the missing safe found?

Free Dog Shampoo Voucher. 001397B
'Mr Diamond' dies peacefully at home
Dan Eagleberg
Count Uself Lukki, the internationally-famous philanthropist, philatelist, and collector of some of the world's most precious of precious gems has died in his sleep at home. He would have been 120 years old next Tuesday.
The late Count acquired his nickname 'Mister Diamond', his wealth and his many different collections by discovering the Lukki Diamond back in 1952.
Count Lukki as a baby
He went on to become one of the world's greatest collectors of everything from diamonds to silk vegetables. It is believed that he has left all of these collections to the Earl E. Byrdd Institute.
Though extremely rich, the Count was in the habit of giving his friends the same gift every year: a sparkling glass paperweight.
He had homes in New York and the capital city of Verstroodl in the Republic of Olanga.
Count Lukki's will 'is missing'
from our legal correspondent
Both copies of the will of billionaire Count Uself Lukki have disappeared according to his lawyer of sixty years, Ms. Gertrude Sparrow. She told reporters "Lukki recently drew up a new will, keeping a copy for himself and giving me one to put in my safe. Unfortunately, his copy cannot be found and neither can my safe."
The lawyer went on to ex
that she was not allowed
what was in the missi
will. "All will be re
will has been re
One line of investigation is that the Black Diamond might have been stolen by the gang of international jewel thieves SNATCH. They are believed to be behind a number of attempted break-ins at the world-famous Black Eag Diamond Mine.
Who stole the Black Diamond?
Police baffled
eems to know what it
ut everyone knows
Lukki's p
of missing
from our own corres
Police investigating the dis
the safe containing the late C
will now suspect that it was sto
villain, Archie Rook. Mr. Rook
the Count's plumber and was m
leak in the office of the Count's la
time of the disappearance o

Sparrow marries Rook
Thurs: Ms. Gertrude Sparrow, lawyer to the la[...] Count Uself [...] yesterday annou[...] married conv[...] Archie Roo[...] Mr. Rook, [...] accused of s[...] containing [...] Lukki will.
Mr. Rook and th[...] Miss Sparrow were [...] at a civil ceremony. "I [...] have been a naughty [...] ut he's a great plumber [...] love him," the newlywe[...] rs. Rook told waitin[...] orters.
'Safe and well'
Tues: Well-known pe[...] crook and plumber Archi[...] Rook is being questioned [...] police regarding the s[...] missing from the offices [...] Miss Gertrude Sparrow.
Miss Sparrow's missing safe [...] was found under [...] Rook's bed when [...] local detectives [...] searched his [...] apartment last night.
Black Diamond missing
The $2\frac{1}{2}$ milli[...] Black Diam[...] mentioned [...] Count L[...] will, is s[...] to hav[...] given [...] E. [...] In[...]
Missing 'Lukki will' found
Dan Eagleberg
A copy of the missing will of the late Count Uself Lukki was found yesterday by his lawyer for almost sixty years, Ms. Gertrude Sparrow. "Silly me! The will was in my handbag all the time." she said. "It was never even in the safe."
As was widely reported, Lukki has left his collections to the Earl E. Byrdd Institute.
Mrs Gertrude Rook (formerly Ms. Sparrow) at a press conference.
Stop Press
Police suspect the SNATCH gang could be behind missing Black Diamond. Sid [...]sty seen near Earl [...]yrdd Institute.
Black Diamond missing
[Th]e most valuable item listed in Count Lukki's will and left to the Earl E. Byrdd Institute is missing. "We can't find it anywhere," says lawyer Gertrude Sparrow. "The Count's instructions were clear. He said to arrange to have Thackery send the Black Diamond along with the original packaging with which he, the Count, first received it from Olanga. The count added that Thackery was an expert and that he would realize the Black Diamond's value and would place it on display at the Institute.'"
Gideon T. Thackery III told reporters "I was amazed to find the package was empty, apart from some tissue paper. The Black Diamond has been stolen!" [A]ll other collections left to the Institute
philanthropist n. a person who performs charitable acts [from Greek philos meaning loving and anthropos meaning man]
philatelist n. a collector and studier of postage stamps [from the French philatélie]
TODAY'S BREAKFAST SPECIA[L]
Orange Juice
*
Grapefruit
*
Cereal
*
Pancakes
*
Toast
*
Coffee
*
Stomachache

Ofppr
Nzib Irxph
Drohlm
Szilow Hnrgs

A COLLECTION OF CLUES

Time: Monday, 12:24pm
Place: Office of Bequests & Acquisitions,
Earl E. Byrdd Institute

The first name on your list of possible suspects is the assistant deputy curator, Gideon T. Thackery III. He's busy right now, so you snoop around this room where they store some of the new collections. Each collection has been coded with the donor's name. No gems here, but there is one of Lukki's other collections.

Which collection was donated by Count Lukki? Who donated the other items?

Ixias pyrene insignis
Qrn Xzigvi
termessus
crocale

A PUZZLING PACKAGE

Time: Monday, 1:03pm
Place: The office of Gideon T. Thackery III,
Earl E. Byrdd Institute

Thackery shows you a box. It was originally used to send the *Black Diamond* to the Count from Olanga. The same box was later sent here, to the institute. "When I opened it, there was nothing in it," says Thackery. When he's called away to speak to someone named Olive, you slink around to his side of the desk.

Any signs of any gems?

Count U. Lukki,
Lukki Tower,
Billionaire Drive,
N.Y., N.Y.

laoreet dolore magna
enim ad minim veniam
sequat UMBRA
"Wisi enim"
Trews 20,000.00

A MYSTERIOUS GIFT

Time: Monday, 3:10pm
Place: The Sidewalk Cafe,
outside New Central Station

Next on the list is Gertrude Rook. You stop for a bite to eat, before catching a train to her office. You squeeze your cake and milkshake onto the corner of a table. It's occupied by a woman hiding behind a newspaper. You're about to sit down, when she pushes a present out from under her paper. "For you," she says "Follow the advice on it. A detective is on our trail."

What does the advice say?

ON THE RIGHT TRACK

Time: Monday, 3:52pm
Place: On a speeding train

You've unwrapped the present to find a red tin box. You empty its contents onto your detective-issue briefcase. In among the items are what appears to be a coded message, some uncut diamonds, a map and a green pass card.

Could the bird be a clue?
Where might it lead you?

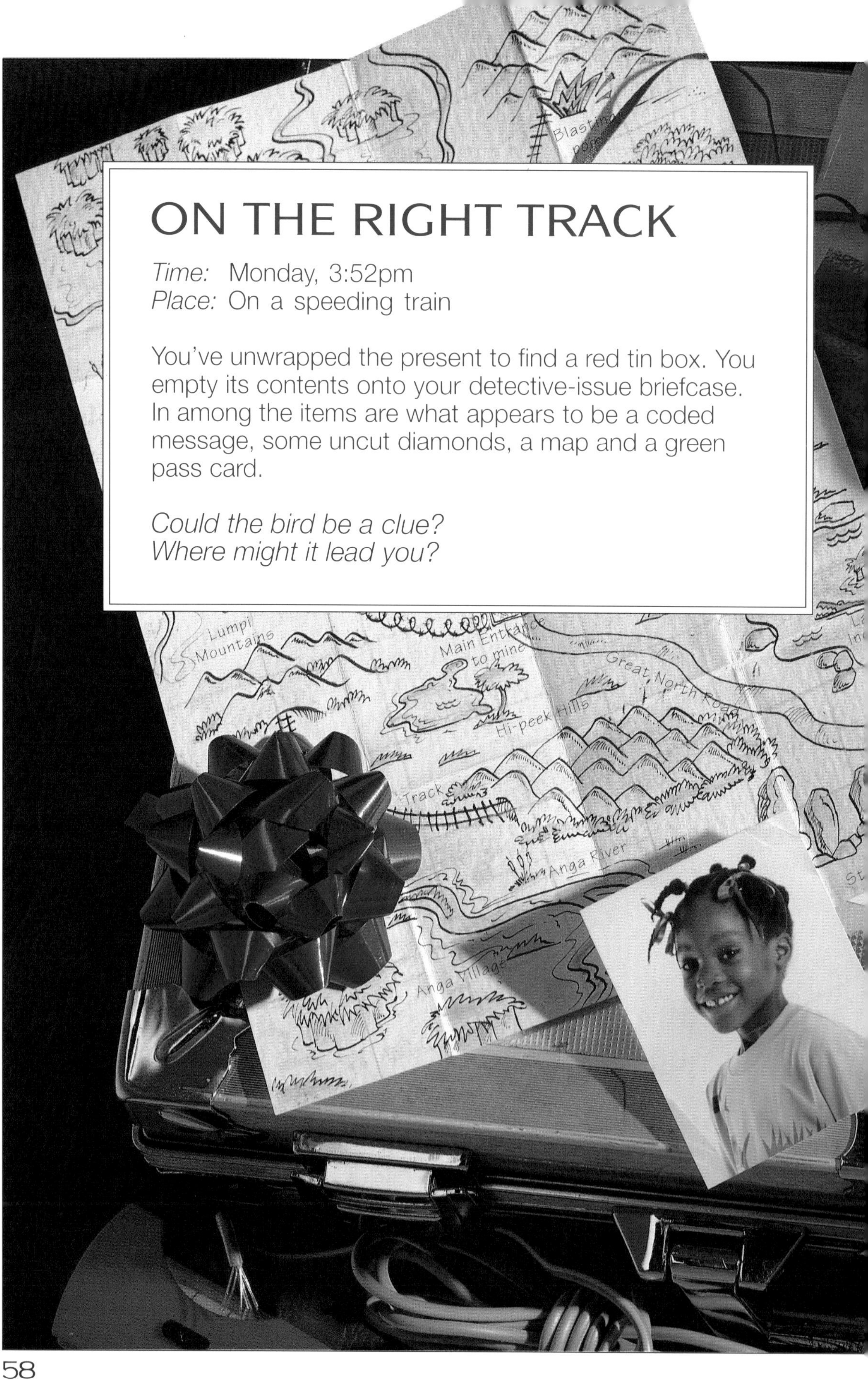

Lumpi Mountains
Main Entrance to mine
Great North Road
Hi-peek Hills
Track
Anga River
Anga Village

MLRRV JOBURF
OXUJOWXYZVU,
AOL RLF VWLUZ
AOL ZPAL
VMMPJL AV
AOL I.L.K.T.
DOHA FVB ULLK
PZ PU AOLYL
ZUHAJO

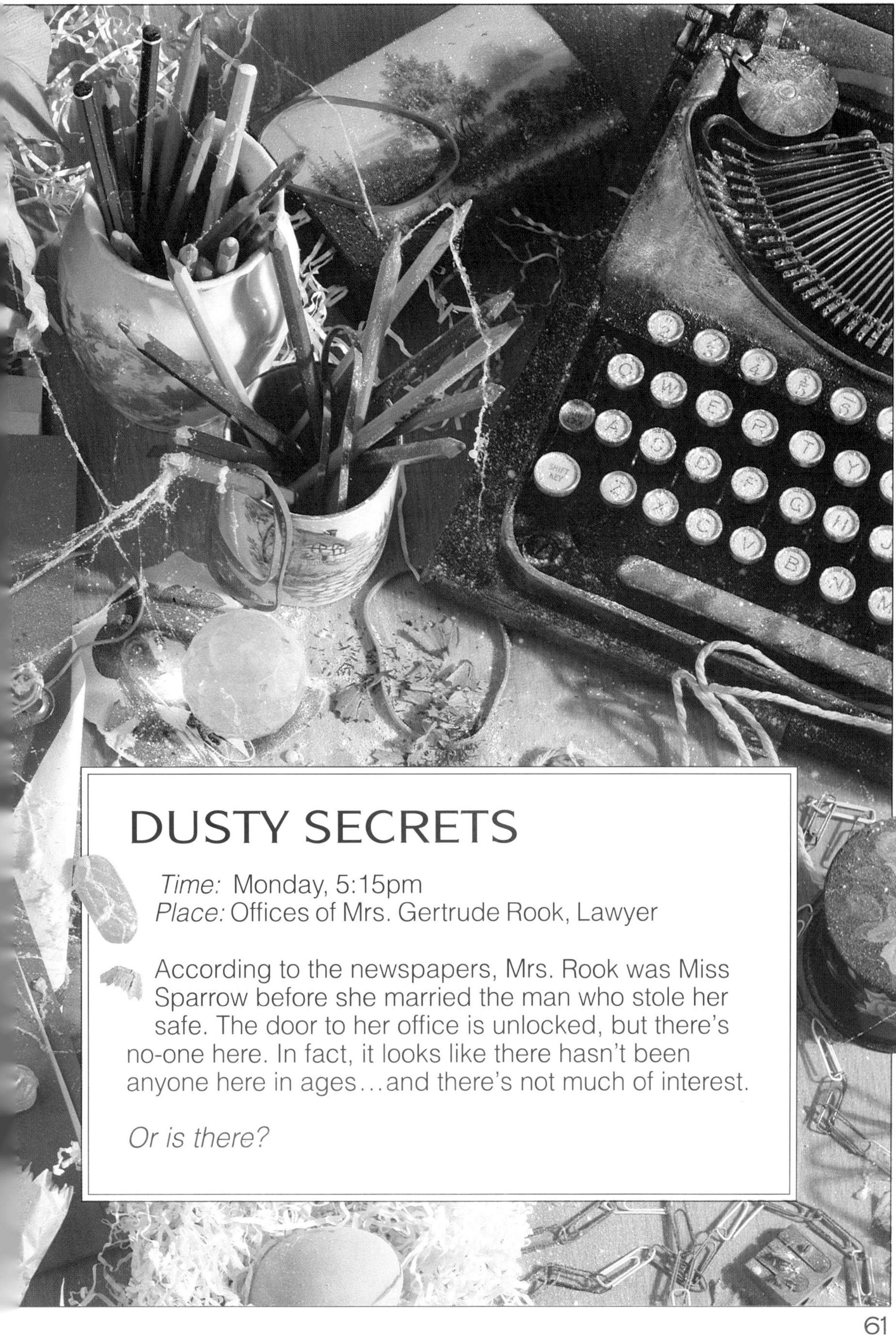

DUSTY SECRETS

Time: Monday, 5:15pm
Place: Offices of Mrs. Gertrude Rook, Lawyer

According to the newspapers, Mrs. Rook was Miss Sparrow before she married the man who stole her safe. The door to her office is unlocked, but there's no-one here. In fact, it looks like there hasn't been anyone here in ages…and there's not much of interest.

Or is there?

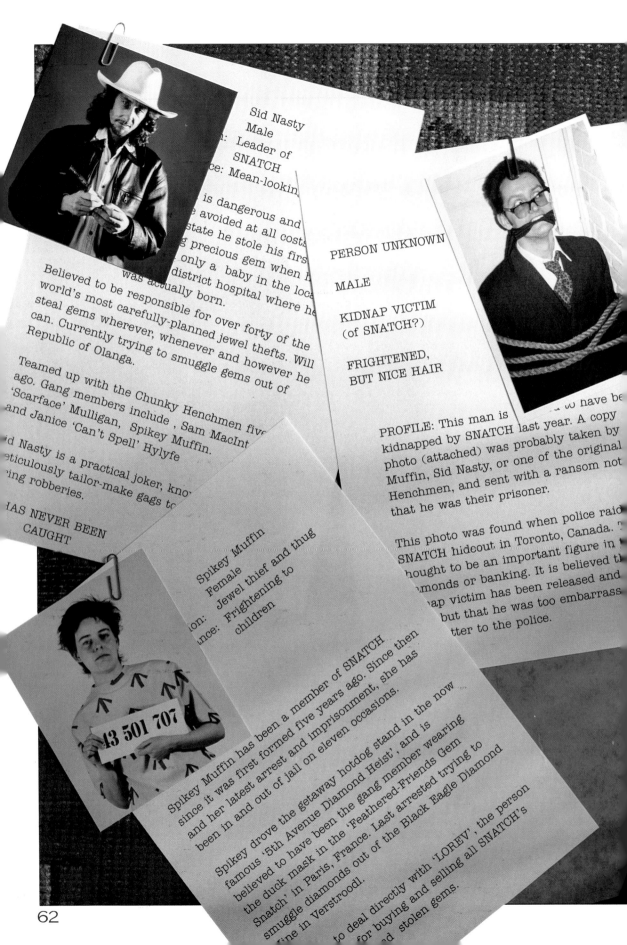

Sid Nasty
Male
n: Leader of SNATCH
ce: Mean-lookin

is dangerous and e avoided at all costs state he stole his firs g precious gem when h only a baby in the loca district hospital where he was actually born.

Believed to be responsible for over forty of the world's most carefully-planned jewel thefts. Will steal gems wherever, whenever and however he can. Currently trying to smuggle gems out of Republic of Olanga.

Teamed up with the Chunky Henchmen five ago. Gang members include , Sam MacInt 'Scarface' Mulligan, Spikey Muffin. and Janice 'Can't Spell' Hylyfe

id Nasty is a practical joker, kno eticulously tailor-make gags to ring robberies.

HAS NEVER BEEN CAUGHT

PERSON UNKNOWN

MALE

KIDNAP VICTIM (of SNATCH?)

FRIGHTENED, BUT NICE HAIR

PROFILE: This man is to have be kidnapped by SNATCH last year. A copy photo (attached) was probably taken by Muffin, Sid Nasty, or one of the original Henchmen, and sent with a ransom not that he was their prisoner.

This photo was found when police raid SNATCH hideout in Toronto, Canada. T hought to be an important figure in t monds or banking. It is believed th ap victim has been released and but that he was too embarrass tter to the police.

43 501 707

Spikey Muffin
Female
ion: Jewel thief and thug
ance: Frightening to children

Spikey Muffin has been a member of SNATCH since it was first formed five years ago. Since then and her latest arrest and imprisonment, she has been in and out of jail on eleven occasions.

Spikey drove the getaway hotdog stand in the now famous '5th Avenue Diamond Heist', and is believed to have been the gang member wearing the duck mask in the 'Feathered-Friends Gem Snatch' in Paris, France. Last arrested trying to smuggle diamonds out of the Black Eagle Diamond ine in Verstroodl.

to deal directly with 'LOREV', the person for buying and selling all SNATCH's d stolen gems.

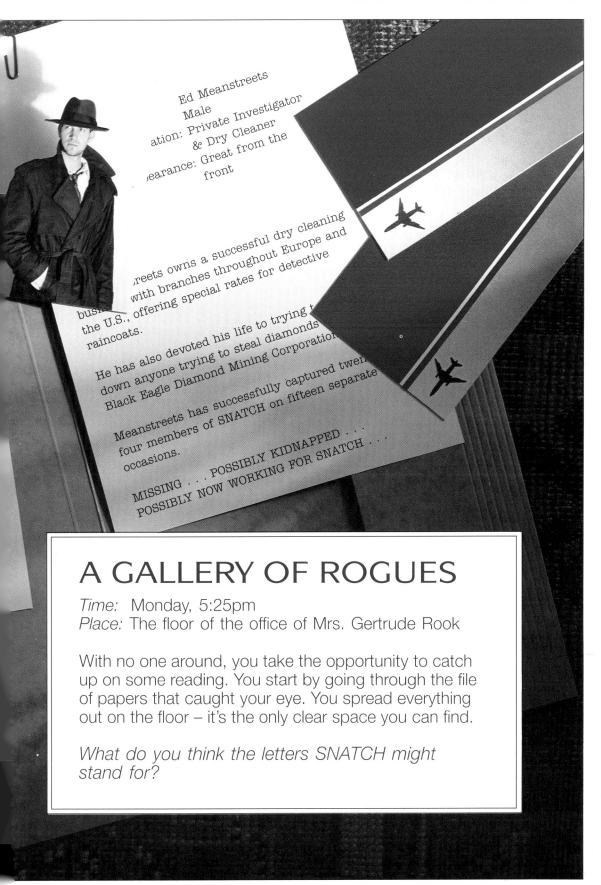

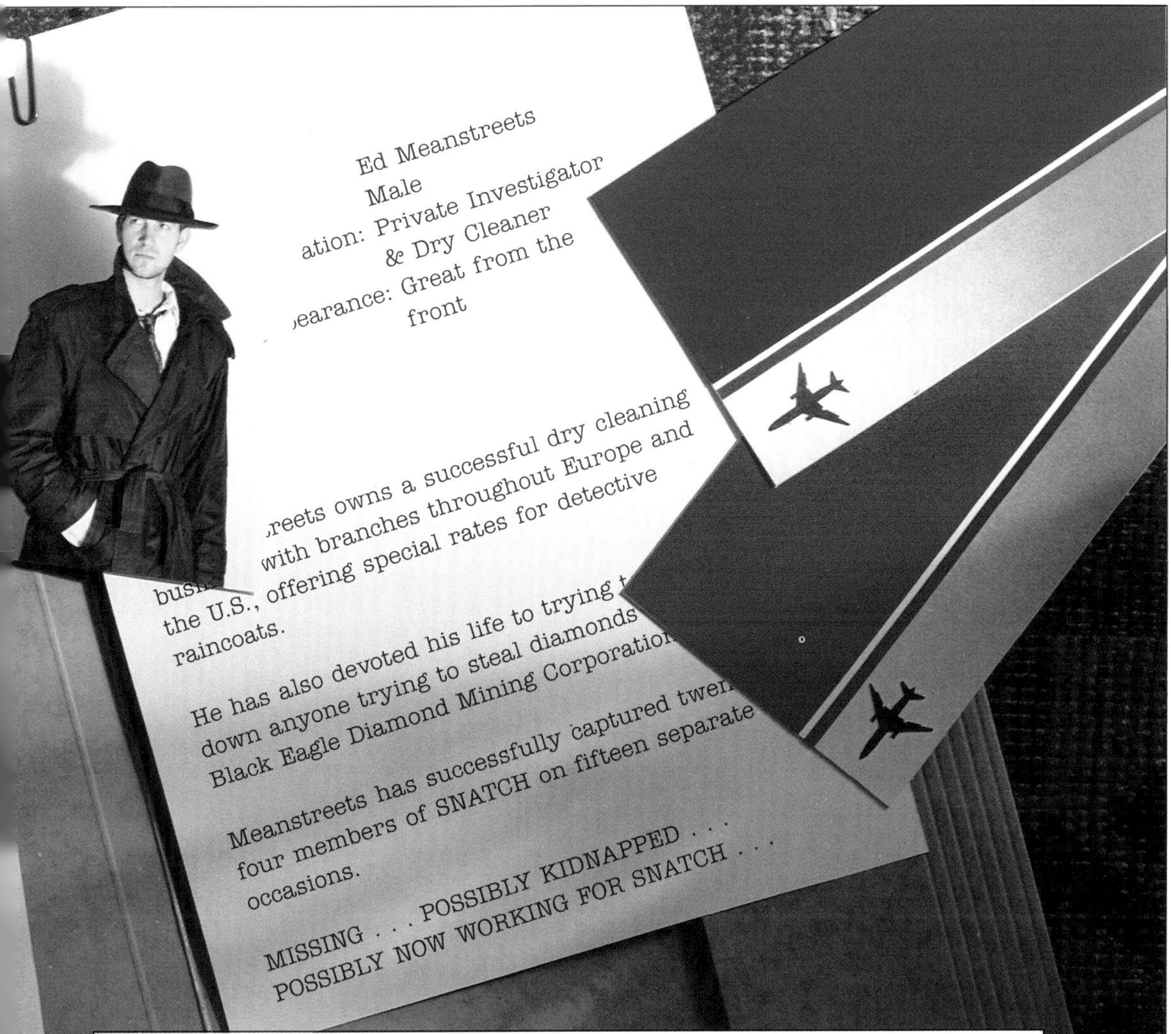
Ed Meanstreets
Male
ation: Private Investigator
& Dry Cleaner
earance: Great from the
front
reets owns a successful dry cleaning
with branches throughout Europe and
the U.S., offering special rates for detective
raincoats.
He has also devoted his life to trying t
down anyone trying to steal diamonds
Black Eagle Diamond Mining Corporatio
Meanstreets has successfully captured twe
four members of SNATCH on fifteen separate
occasions.
MISSING . . . POSSIBLY KIDNAPPED . . .
POSSIBLY NOW WORKING FOR SNATCH . . .

A GALLERY OF ROGUES

Time: Monday, 5:25pm
Place: The floor of the office of Mrs. Gertrude Rook

With no one around, you take the opportunity to catch up on some reading. You start by going through the file of papers that caught your eye. You spread everything out on the floor – it's the only clear space you can find.

What do you think the letters SNATCH might stand for?

GLITTERING PRIZES

Time: Wednesday, 10:30am
Place: Workshop, 1st Floor,
Hans Anderfeet Diamond Merchants

It's time to speak to Christen Hans Anderfeet, down on the list as a 'diamond expert'. Sitting at his workbench, he claims to know nothing about the *Black Diamond* in particular or Olangan jewels in general. "I never use any stones from the Republic of Olanga," he says.

Do you believe him?

SPILLING THE BEANS

Time: Wednesday, 1:15pm
Place: Foyer, *Hotel New Amsterdam*

You've been followed by a woman since you left the diamond merchant and now she's shadowed you back to your hotel. You bump into her to see if she panics. Instead, she drops her bag and everything spills out. Nothing much here, but that key-ring looks rather interesting, and what about that photo? The dreadful rhyme is certainly good news.

Why and how?

Fellow henchmen
and henchwomen:
If you take my eye
to be your bee
The rest is simple,
you'll agree.
It will make my jay
your sea
And later make
my bee be you.
Don't believe me?
Try. It's true.

J.T. 0
S.M. 0 1 1 2
S.N. 1 1 2 2

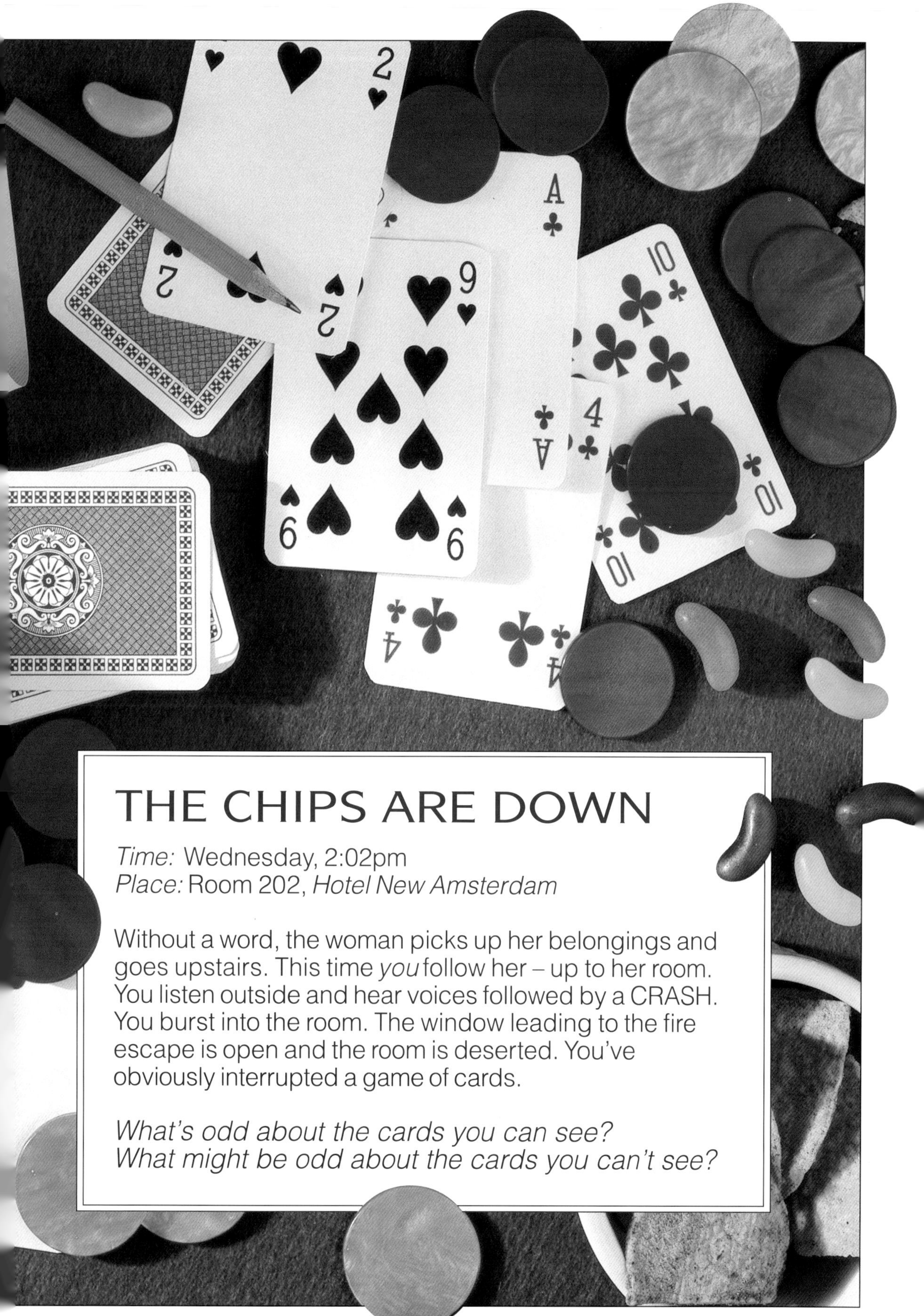

THE CHIPS ARE DOWN

Time: Wednesday, 2:02pm
Place: Room 202, *Hotel New Amsterdam*

Without a word, the woman picks up her belongings and goes upstairs. This time *you* follow her – up to her room. You listen outside and hear voices followed by a CRASH. You burst into the room. The window leading to the fire escape is open and the room is deserted. You've obviously interrupted a game of cards.

What's odd about the cards you can see?
What might be odd about the cards you can't see?

ROOM SERVICE

Time: Wednesday, 2:34pm
Place: Room 234, *Hotel New Amsterdam*

You go back to your own room to find that the place has been searched from top to bottom. Even your toothpaste tube has been emptied. A far from friendly message is stuck to your pillow with a hatpin. But that's not all that your unwelcome intruder has left behind.

What telltale clues suggest the identity of the unwelcome visitor?

YOU WERE
GIVUN THE MAP AND
MESSAGE BY MISTEAK.
GO BACK HOME AND
FORGET THE BLACK
DIMOND OR ELSE.
TAKE MY ADVICE
YOU HAVE BEAN
WARMED.

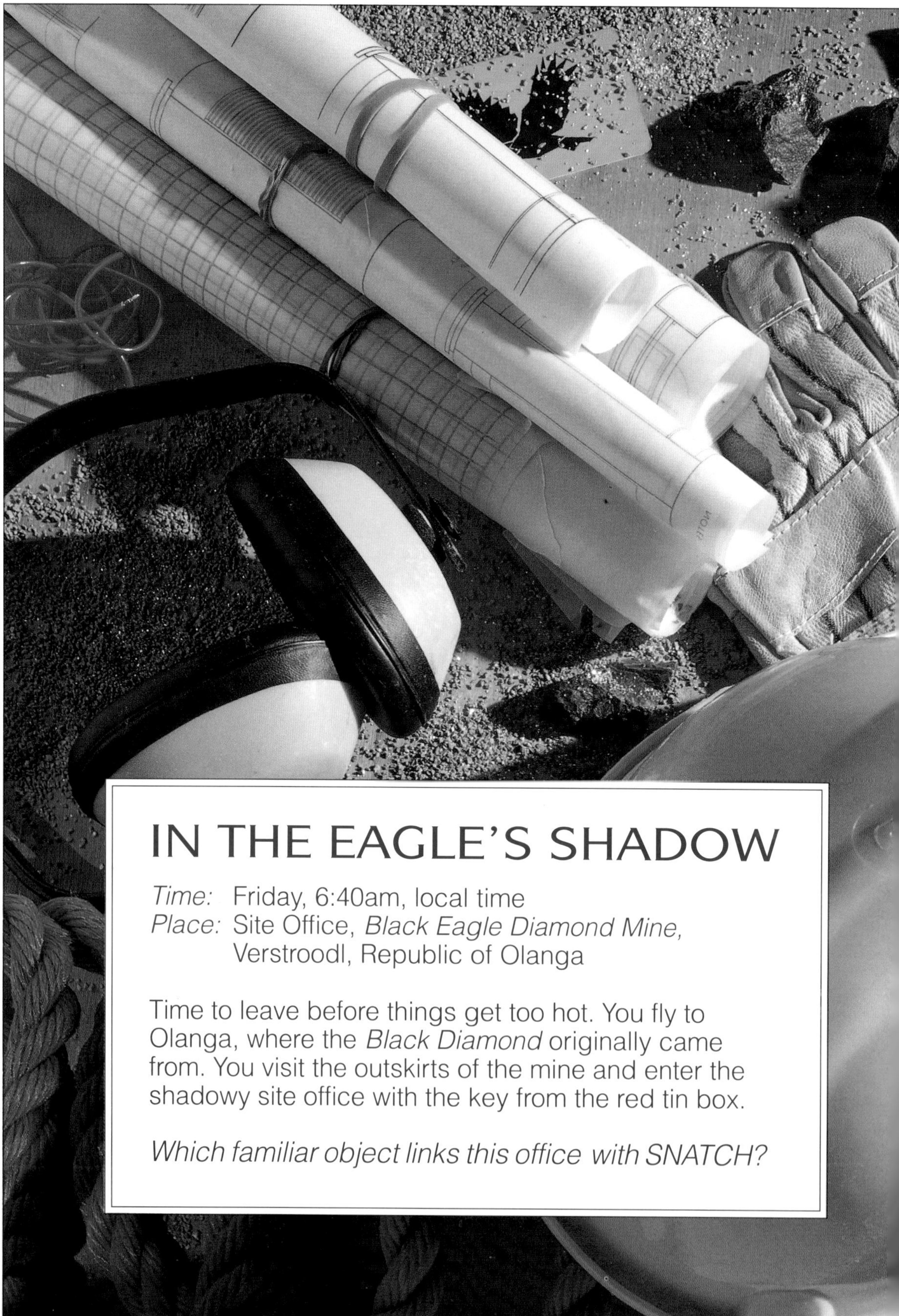

IN THE EAGLE'S SHADOW

Time: Friday, 6:40am, local time
Place: Site Office, *Black Eagle Diamond Mine,* Verstroodl, Republic of Olanga

Time to leave before things get too hot. You fly to Olanga, where the *Black Diamond* originally came from. You visit the outskirts of the mine and enter the shadowy site office with the key from the red tin box.

Which familiar object links this office with SNATCH?

UNDER ARREST

Time: Friday, 8:11am
Place: Captain Appul's Office,
Verstroodl Police Headquarters, Olanga

Caught snooping by the local cops, you've been taken in for questioning. The phone rings and the captain leaves you alone for a moment. You may be handcuffed, but you can still use your eyes. The drawer in his desk is open, so who can blame you for taking a peep?

What vital piece of information lurks among the mess?

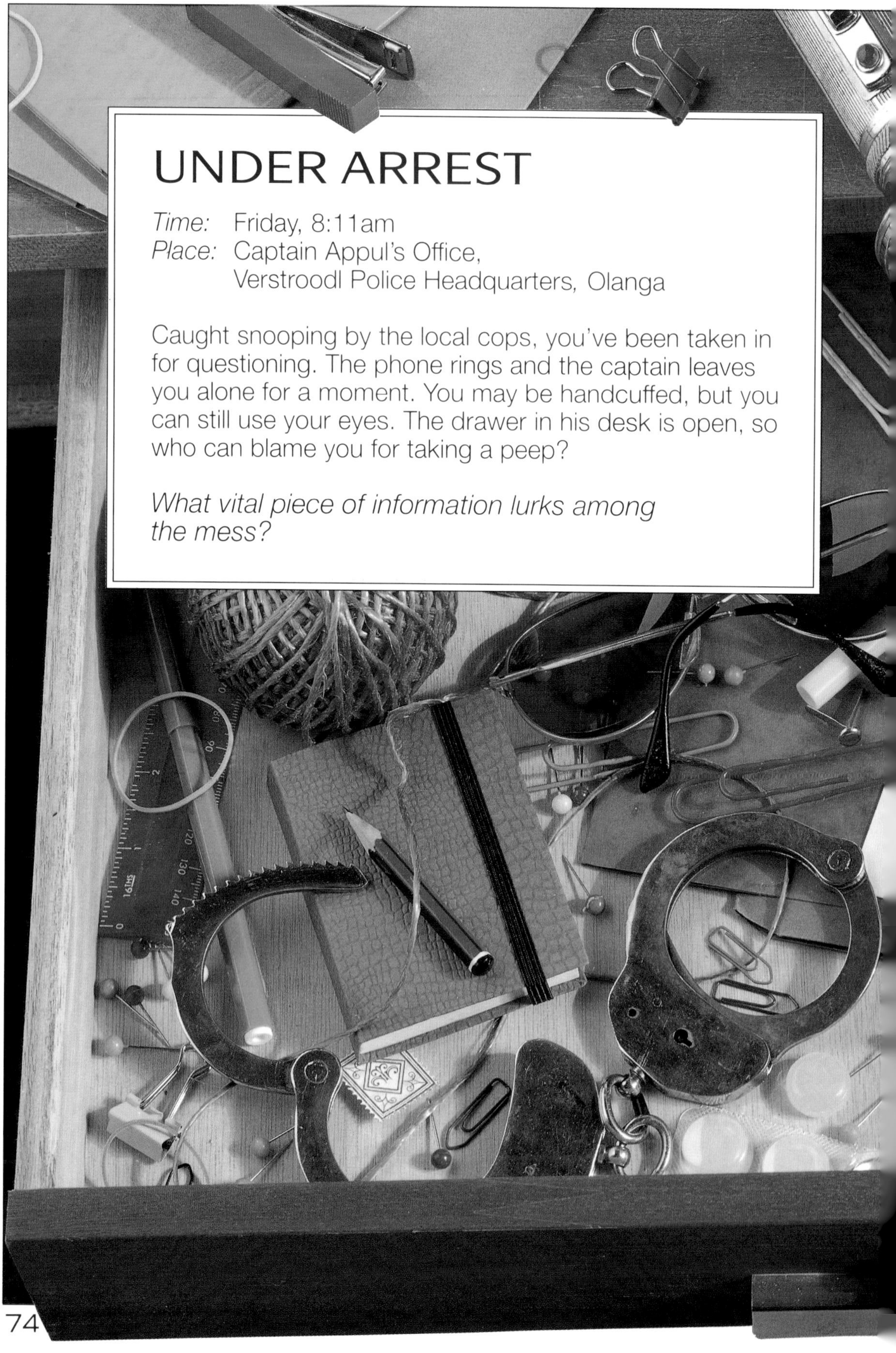

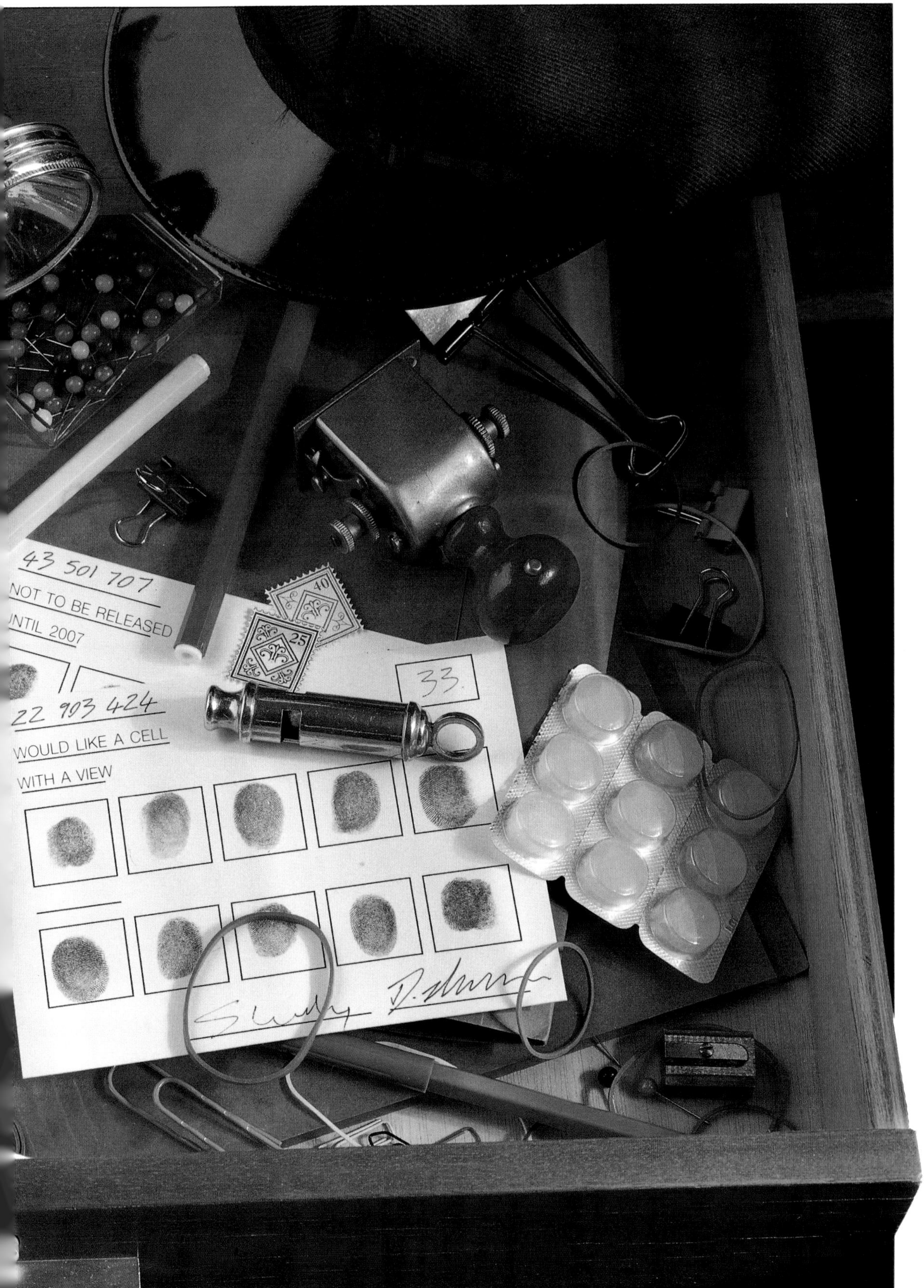
43 501 707
NOT TO BE RELEASED
UNTIL 2007
22 903 424
WOULD LIKE A CELL
WITH A VIEW
33.
40
25

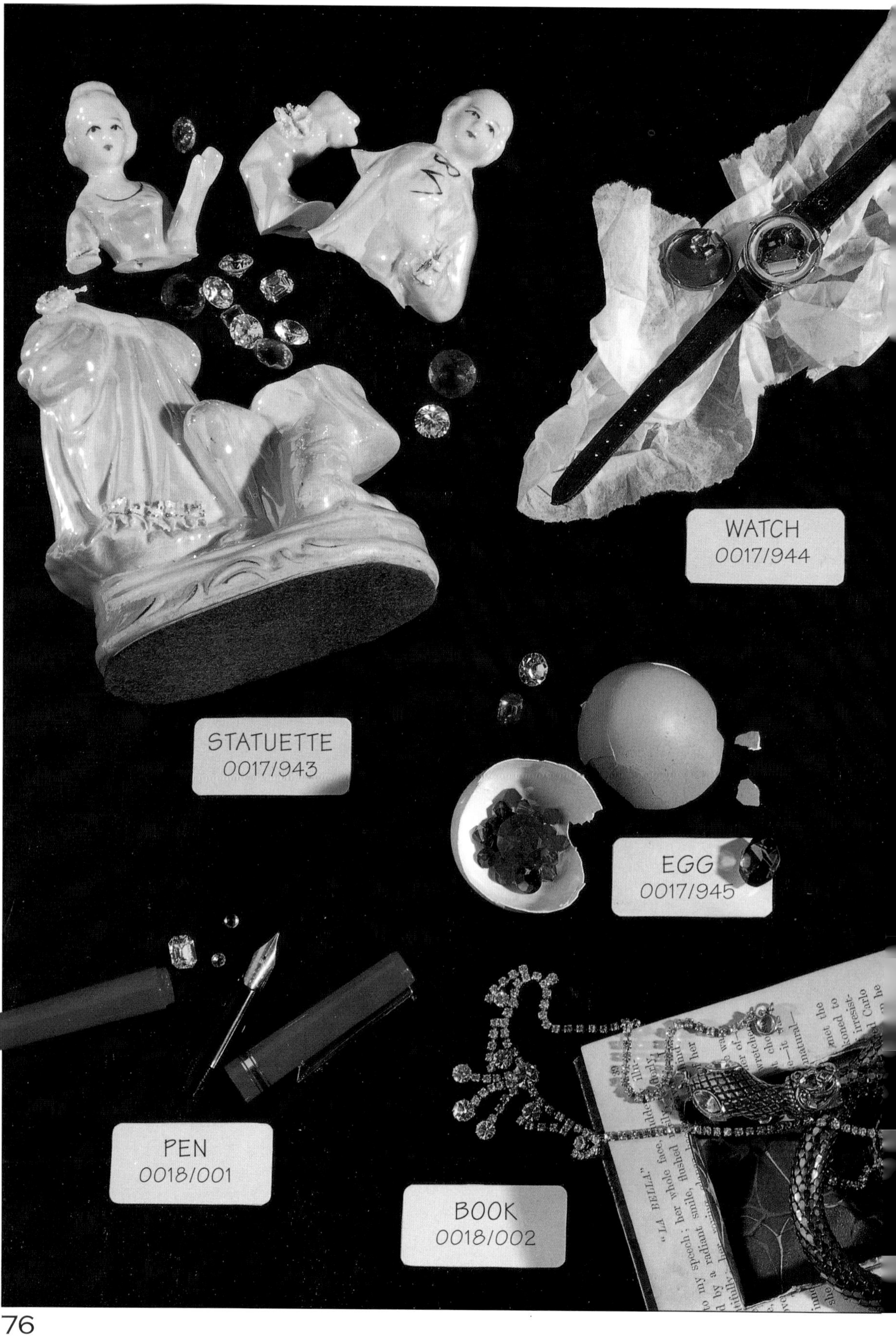

WATCH
0017/944
STATUETTE
0017/943
EGG
0017/945
PEN
0018/001
BOOK
0018/002

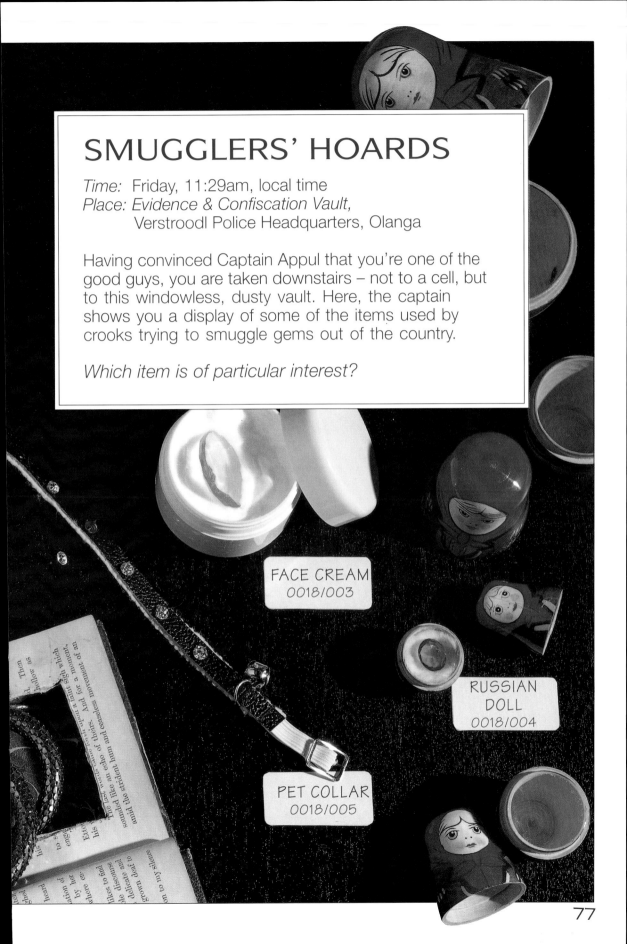

SMUGGLERS' HOARDS

Time: Friday, 11:29am, local time
Place: Evidence & Confiscation Vault,
Verstroodl Police Headquarters, Olanga

Having convinced Captain Appul that you're one of the good guys, you are taken downstairs – not to a cell, but to this windowless, dusty vault. Here, the captain shows you a display of some of the items used by crooks trying to smuggle gems out of the country.

Which item is of particular interest?

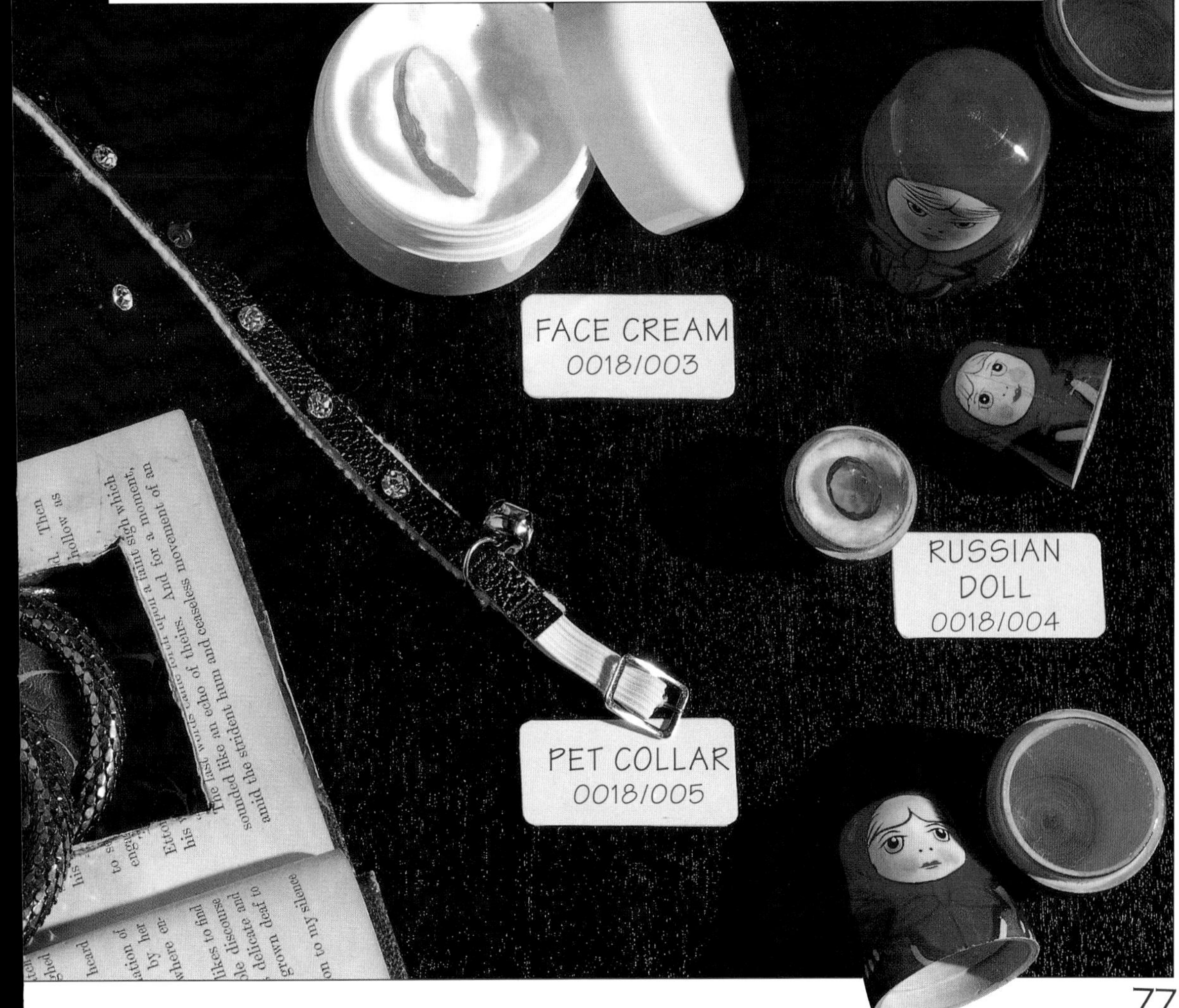
FACE CREAM
0018/003
RUSSIAN DOLL
0018/004
PET COLLAR
0018/005

That is why this carbon-based fuel (not shown here) is sometimes referred to as black diamond.
It is the most widely burned fossil fuel in Olanga.
NOTE: Rocks shown here relate to text on page 23.
- 24 -
ALL STAFF ARE INVITED TO PROFESSOR POFFLE'S "BRING-A-ROCK PARTY"
THIS FRIDAY.
MINERAL WATER WILL BE PROVIDED
extremely viscous.
gases cause massive
to occur as they
During the explosions.
amounts of volcanic ash are
thrown high into the air.
One type of movement at plate boundaries involves one plate plunging below another. Some scientists think this sets off all the other movements. At some boundaries, molten rock rises between two plates.
This hardens onto the plate edges, pushing the plates apart. this may set off all other plate movement. [See page 156.]
The Big Yawn Coal Mine Fact Sheet 11
Diamond is made from carbon and coal is too – but its carbon atoms are arranged differently. That is why one is a sparkling gem and the other is the most commonly used fossil fuel in Olanga.
Wheelhouse
of the staff canteen has instructed that no further meals will be served until scientists stop hiding minerals in the rock cakes.

IN THE LABORATORY

Time: Friday, 1:55pm, local time
Place: Geology Lab, Scientific Department,
Black Eagle Mining Corporation

While you're in Olanga, you visit the 6th person on your list – Dr. Robin Swyne-Thevin. He claims to know nothing about Count Lukki's particular *Black Diamond*, but plenty about 'black diamonds' in general. He even claims to have a black diamond in his lab!

If so, where is it?

Fig 1.
A rock
Fig 94.
Yet another rock
Fig 95.
You guessed it, a rock again.
- 68 -
LOST
Black & white
cat called
DIAMOND.
If found,
contact

HATS OFF TO PERCY

Time: Monday, 10:00am precisely
Place: The manager's outer office,
Snoots & Co Bank, London, England

Now it's off to London. You're waiting to be shown into the manager's inner office. It was he who originally arranged to ship the *Black Diamond* from Olanga to Count Lukki back in 1990. There's not much to look at apart from the hats and scarfs hanging on the wall . . . but there's something here that's naggingly familiar.

What is it?

CO BANK
Smart
43718

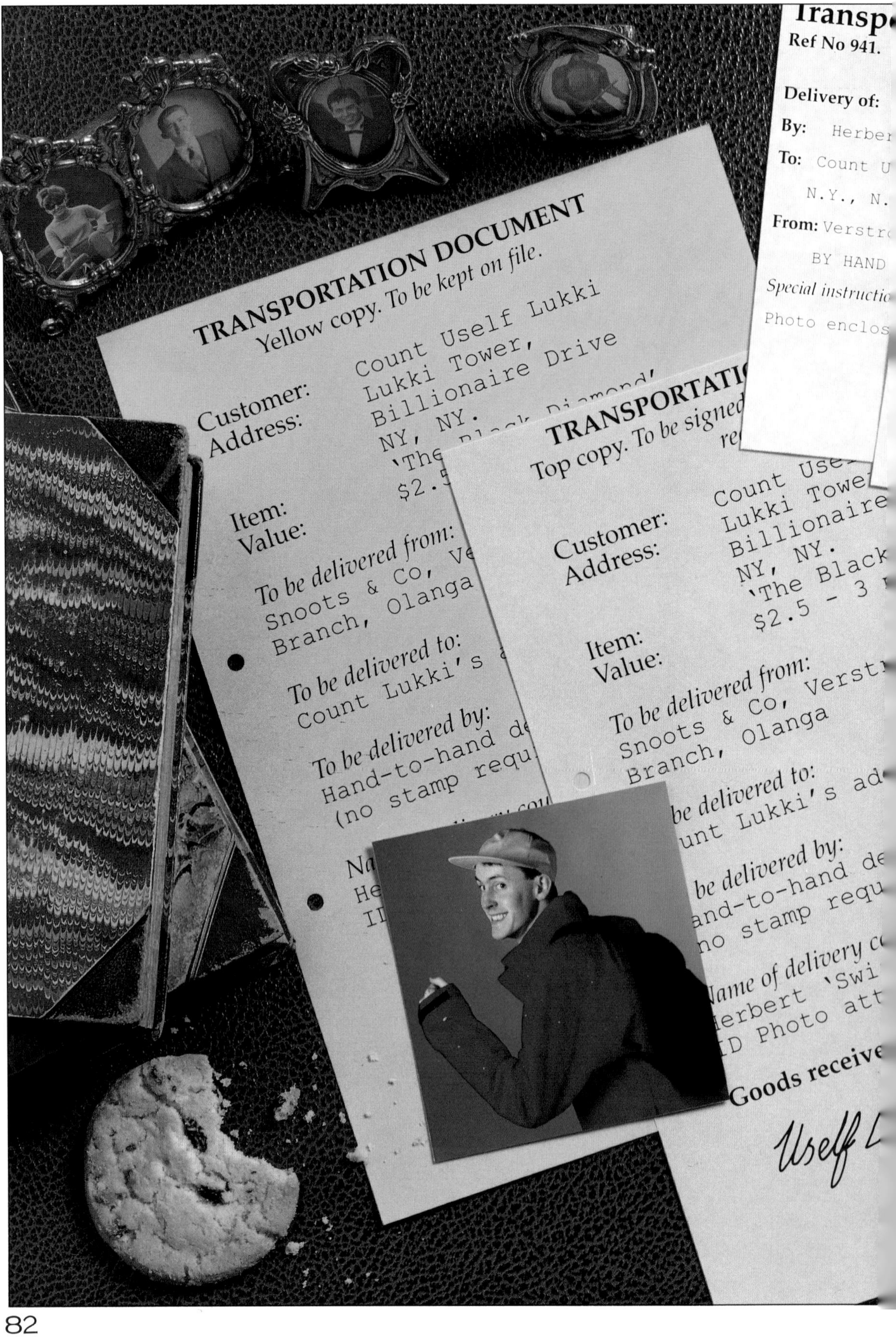
Transp
Ref No 941.
Delivery of:
By: Herber
To: Count U
N.Y., N.
From: Verstr
BY HAND
Special instructi
Photo enclos
TRANSPORTATION DOCUMENT
Yellow copy. To be kept on file.
Customer: Count Uself Lukki
Address: Lukki Tower,
Billionaire Drive
NY, NY.
Item:
Value:
To be delivered from:
Snoots & Co, Ve
Branch, Olanga
To be delivered to:
Count Lukki's a
To be delivered by:
Hand-to-hand de
(no stamp requi
TRANSPORTATI
Top copy. To be signed
Customer: Count Use
Address: Lukki Towe
Billionaire
NY, NY.
'The Black
Item:
Value: $2.5 - 3
To be delivered from:
Snoots & Co, Verst
Branch, Olanga
be delivered to:
unt Lukki's ad
be delivered by:
and-to-hand de
no stamp requ
Name of delivery c
Herbert 'Swi
ID Photo att
Goods receive
Uself L

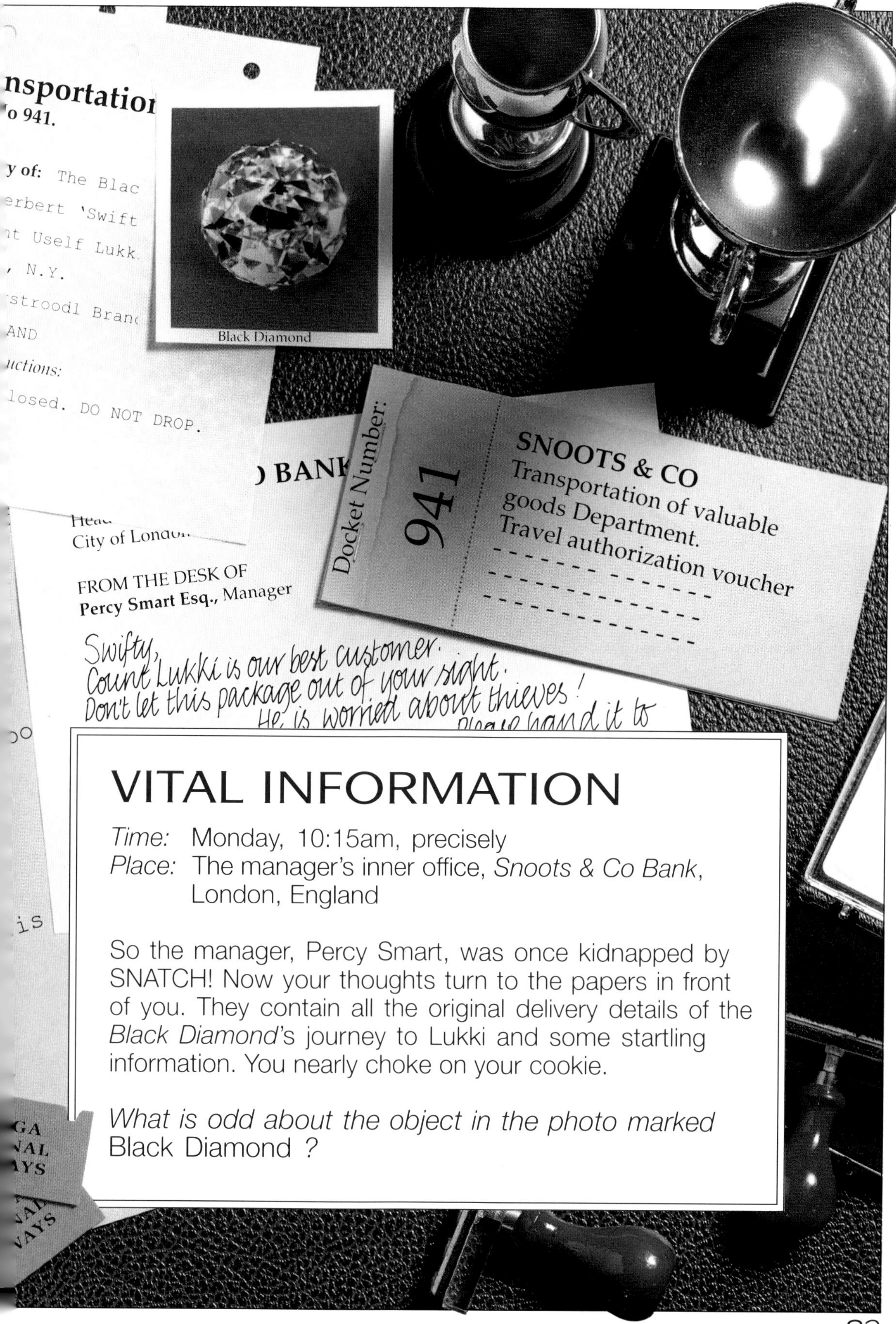

Black Diamond
DO NOT DROP.
Docket Number:
941
SNOOTS & CO
Transportation of valuable goods Department.
Travel authorization voucher
FROM THE DESK OF
Percy Smart Esq., Manager
Swifty,
Count Lukki is our best customer.
Don't let this package out of your sight.
He is worried about thieves!

VITAL INFORMATION

Time: Monday, 10:15am, precisely
Place: The manager's inner office, *Snoots & Co Bank*, London, England

So the manager, Percy Smart, was once kidnapped by SNATCH! Now your thoughts turn to the papers in front of you. They contain all the original delivery details of the *Black Diamond*'s journey to Lukki and some startling information. You nearly choke on your cookie.

What is odd about the object in the photo marked Black Diamond *?*

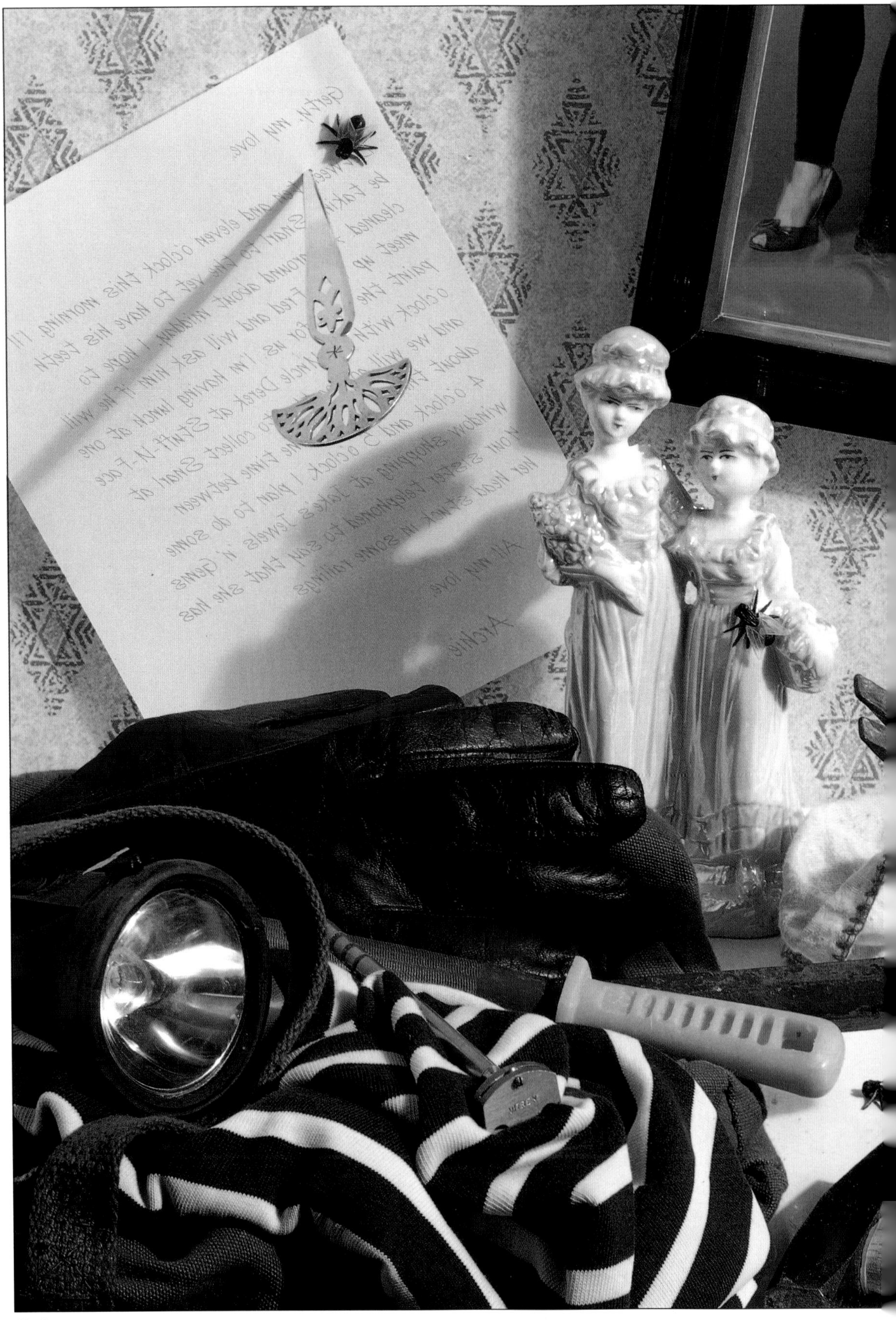
Gerty, my love,
and eleven o'clock this morning I'll
Snarl to the vet to have his teeth
cleaned
around about midday I hope to
meet up
Fred and will ask him if he will
paint the
for us. I'm having lunch at one
o'clock with
Uncle Derek at Stuff-N-Face
and we will
to collect Snarl at
about
the time between
4 o'clock and 5 o'clock I plan to do some
window shopping at Jake's Jewels 'n' Gems
Your sister telephoned to say that she has
her head stuck in some railings
All my love
Archie

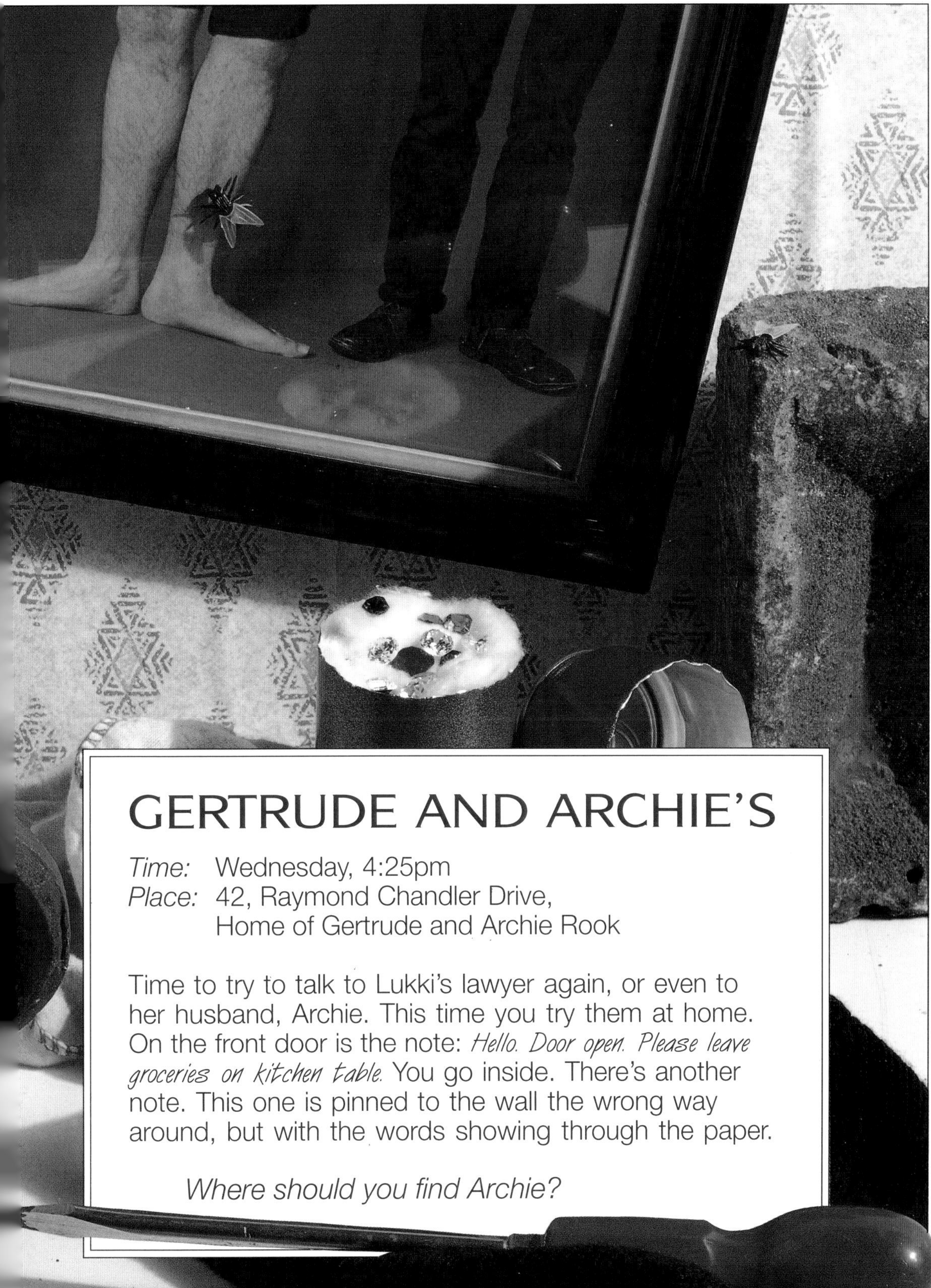

GERTRUDE AND ARCHIE'S

Time: Wednesday, 4:25pm
Place: 42, Raymond Chandler Drive,
Home of Gertrude and Archie Rook

Time to try to talk to Lukki's lawyer again, or even to her husband, Archie. This time you try them at home. On the front door is the note: *Hello. Door open. Please leave groceries on kitchen table.* You go inside. There's another note. This one is pinned to the wall the wrong way around, but with the words showing through the paper.

Where should you find Archie?

QUALITY JEWELS
AT GIVEAWAY PRICES

Great sale
today.
Everything
must go!
JAKE'S JEWELS & GEMS

SMASH 'N' GRAB

Time: Wednesday, 4:50pm
Place: Outside *Jake's Jewels 'n' Gems*

Archie Rook's message brings you to the right place, but a little late. You're greeted by a broken window. Archie's 'appointment' was a smash and grab raid! There aren't many jewels remaining, but something far more significant has been left at the scene of the crime.

Who does it belong to?

FOOD FOR THOUGHT

Time: Wednesday, 8:00pm
Place: The late Count Uself Lukki's apartment, New York, New York

You end your mission at the home of 'Mr. Diamond' himself. You have a typed list of the suspects in front of you, surrounded by one collection the Count didn't leave to any institute – a rare selection of silk fruit and vegetables. You should now have enough information to answer this key question before turning to page 96:

Who stole the Black Diamond?

SUSPECTS
T. Thackery III / Earl E. Byrdd Institute
AN IMPORTANT REMINDER TO THE READER
To solve this mystery, you need to do more than simply answer the questions asked throughout your mission. There are many other vital clues lying around the place, often where you least expect them. By now, there should be questions you'll want to ask yourself about who stole the Black Diamond.
Take the information you have and use your powers of detective deduction and reasoning to fill in any blanks. Even the police deal in probabilities when catching crooks. In other words, they use guesswork – but it's guesswork based on solid, logical reasoning.
Remember: Count Lukki was a collector of a great many different things.
All sorts of diamonds appear throughout this case, from playing cards to diamond-shaped floor tiles.
Being a liar doesn't necessarily make that person a thief.

HELPFUL HINTS

Pages 50 & 51
The answers are there in black and white. Read everything carefully.

Pages 52 & 53
The labels are in the Earl E. Byrdd Institute's catalogue code. This uses a reverse alphabet running from Z-A.

Pages 54 & 55
Don't forget the framed photos.

Pages 56 & 57
Turn the parcel the right way up and try tackling the bottom right hand corner first.

Pages 58 & 59
The bird looks like an eagle. Wasn't there something about an eagle in one of the newspaper clippings?

Pages 60 & 61
Check the symbols on the files carefully.

Pages 62 & 63
Sid Nasty's initials are S.N. and the 'A' of SNATCH could be for 'And'... but 'Sid Nasty And' whom? The answer is in the documents somewhere.

Pages 64 & 65
Look again. The answer lies in the uncut diamonds.

Pages 66 & 67
Read out loud, some of the words sound like letters. Could this be the key to an earlier message?

Pages 68 & 69
Compare these cards with the ones on Thackery's desk (pages 54 & 55).

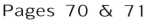

Pages 70 & 71
The intruder is bad at spelling. Hmmm. He, or she, has also dropped something you've seen before.

Pages 72 & 73
The answer lies on the card table back at the *Hotel New Amsterdam*.

Pages 74 & 75
Check the prisoner numbers on the fingerprint cards against any other prisoner numbers you might have seen.

Pages 76 & 77
You've seen one of them before.

60
POLSKA

Pages 78 & 79
The answer is somewhere in those notices.

Pages 80 & 81
You've seen him in another photograph, but he didn't look so happy then.

Pages 82 & 83
You've already seen two objects that look very like it. Can you remember where?

Pages 84 & 85
Read the note Archie has pinned to the wall the wrong way around. You'll get it in time.

Pages 86 & 87
That nail picker looks familiar.

Pages 88 & 89
These are Count Lukki's books. Anything to do with his collections?

ANSWERS

Pages 50 & 51

The answer to both these questions can be found on page 3, in the newspaper article entitled **'Safe and well'**. The *Black Diamond* is worth $2.5m. The missing safe was found under Archie Rook's bed.

Pages 52 & 53

Count Lukki's name has two Ks in it. The only label with two identical letters next to each other is the one attached to the stamp album. It reads 'Ofppr', so, presumably, O=L, F=U, P=K and R=I.
The labels were encoded at the Institute by writing out the alphabet, then, underneath, writing the alphabet in reverse, like this:

A B C D E F G H I J K L M N O P Q R S T U V W X Y Z
Z Y X W V U T S R Q P O N M L K J I H G F E D C B A

Each letter in the top row stands for the letter directly below it. Using this code, 'LUKKI' matches up with 'OFPPR'. The count therefore must have donated the stamp album. Using the same key to decode the other labels, you'll find that the medals were donated by someone called HAROLD SMITH, the butterflies by WILSON, the coins by JIM CARTER and the plants by MARY RICKS.

Pages 54 & 55

There is the large gem-like paperweight on the desk by the photograph of Gideon T. Thackery III and his wife. She is wearing jewels. The cat in the other photograph also appears to be wearing jewels – a diamond-studded collar.

Pages 56 & 57

The writing is in English, but with the letters divided into groups of five instead of words, and the message starting in the bottom right hand corner instead of the top left. With punctuation, the advice reads: **NOT TO BE OPENED WITH ANYONE ELSE AROUND. O.K.?**

Pages 58 & 59

The black bird on the green swipe card is an eagle. The eight stones on the box are uncut diamonds. The map appears to be of a mine. There was a *Black Eagle Diamond Mine* mentioned in one of the newspaper clippings on pages 50 & 51.

Pages 60 & 61

Yes. This file has the same symbol on it as the 'swipe card'.

Pages 62 & 63

SNATCH, the international jewel thief gang, stands for **S**id **N**asty **A**nd **T**he **C**hunky **H**enchmen. In Nasty's profile, it mentions that he joined up with the Chunky Henchmen five years ago.

Pages 64 & 65

The black zip bag full of uncut diamonds obviously comes from the *Black Eagle Diamond Mine*. You can see part of the eagle symbol showing through. You know that the mine is in Verstroodl from the report on Spikey Muffin in Gertrude Rook's office on pages 14 & 15. You know from the newspaper clippings on pages 50 & 51 that Verstroodl is in Olanga. These stones must come from Olanga. Therefore Christen Hans Anderfeet must be lying.

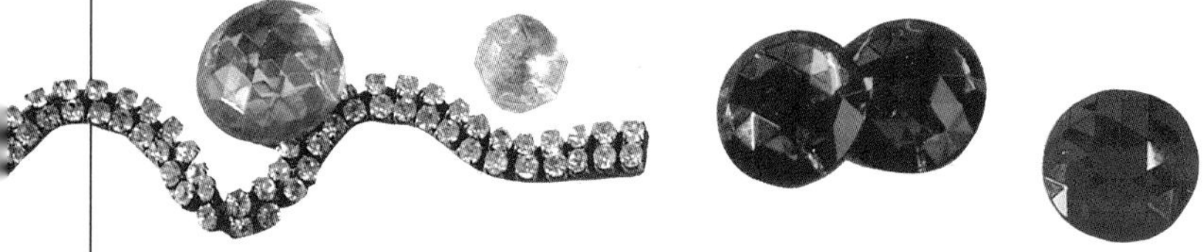

Pages 66 & 67

This poem is the key to a code. It tells us which letters to substitute for which. '**If you take my eye to be your bee**' means that, when decoding a message, the letter 'i' becomes 'b'. It goes on to say that '**It will make my jay your sea**'. This means that the letter 'j' will be decoded as a 'c'. '**And later make my bee be you**' means that the letter 'b' should be decoded as a letter 'u'.

To find out all the other letters of the code, you have to find a sequence which fits in with the letters you already know. The top row represents the letters in the message, and the bottom row the letters which they stand for.

A	B	C	D	E	F	G	H	I	J	K	L	M	N	O	P	Q	R	S	T	U	V	W	X	Y	Z
T	U	V	W	X	Y	Z	A	B	C	D	E	F	G	H	I	J	K	L	M	N	O	P	Q	R	S

With this, you can now decode the message from the red tin box which the woman gave you gift-wrapped at the cafe on pages 56 & 57.

The decoded message reads: **The Key Opens the Site Office to the B.E.D.M. What You Need is in there. SNATCH.**
'**B.E.D.M.**' must stand for the *Black Eagle Diamond Mine*.

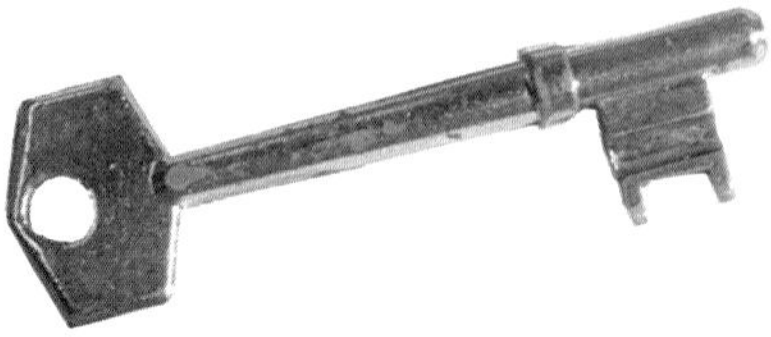

Pages 68 & 69

Cards come in four suits: clubs, spades, hearts and diamonds. With cards from an ordinary pack – such as those on Gideon T. Thackery III's desk on pages 54 & 55 – clubs and spades are black, and hearts and diamonds are red. What's odd about the cards we can see on this table is that the clubs and spades are red, and the hearts are black. This suggests that the missing cards have *black diamonds* on them.

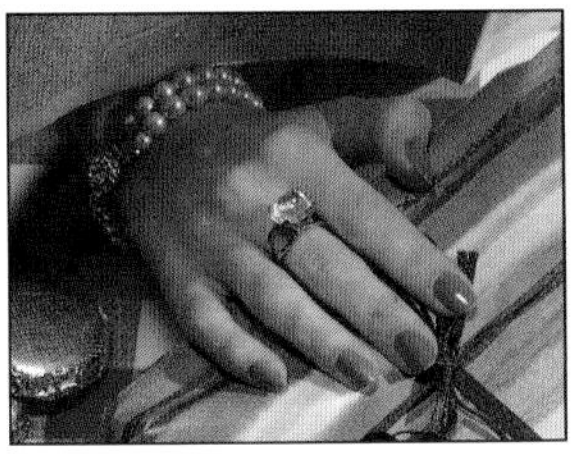

Pages 70 & 71

There is a diamond ring lying in the folds of the bedclothes. You've seen the ring on the finger of the woman who slipped you the package on pages 56 & 57. Then there is the spelling in the note. It's very bad.

The card players who dashed away from Room 202 are most likely to be members of SNATCH. The weird playing cards tie in with Sid Nasty's practical jokes and sense of fun. The initials S.N. on the scorepad are most likely his. According to information in one of the reports in Gertrude Rook's office (on pages 62 & 63) another member of SNATCH is named '**Janice 'Can't Spell' Hylyfe**'. So perhaps Janice Hylyfe, the woman who has been following you, the woman who gave you the package, and the woman who left the badly-spelled note are all one and the same.

Pages 72 & 73

There was a similar red and silver can lying on the card table in Room 202 of the *Hotel New Amsterdam* on pages 68 & 69.

Pages 74 & 75

The bottom fingerprint card has the numbers '43 501 707' on it. These match the prison number held up by Spikey Muffin in her photograph on pages 62 & 63. Written on the fingerprint card are the words 'NOT TO BE RELEASED UNTIL THE YEAR 2007', which means that Spikey Muffin must still be in jail from when the photo was taken . . . and will be for a long time. Because the files in Gertrude Rook's office were so dusty, they must have been lying there for quite a while, and so must the photo . . . this suggests that Spikey Muffin has already been behind bars for some time. This means that the initials 'S.M.' on the pad on the card table (pages 68 & 69) could belong to Sam MacIntosh or 'Scarface' Mulligan (pages 62 & 63).

43 501 707

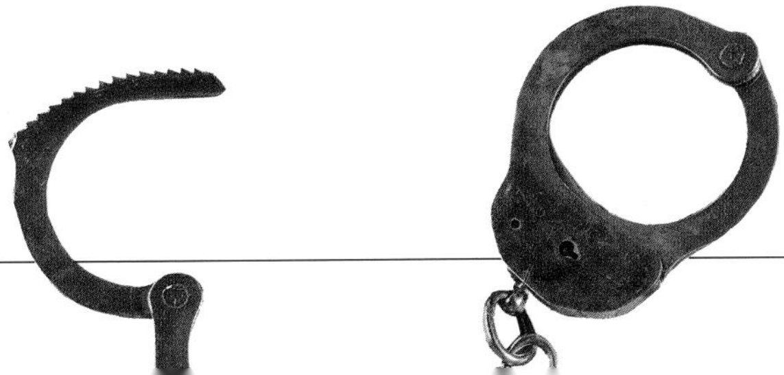

Pages 76 & 77

The diamond-studded pet collar looks familiar. On Gideon T. Thackery III's desk, back at the Earl E. Byrdd Institute, there is a framed photograph of his cat wearing a similar collar. Could it be the *same* collar?

Pages 78 & 79

Yes, one of the pages on the board reads '... that is why this carbon-based fuel . . . is sometimes referred to as 'black diamond'. It is the most widely burned fossil fuel in Olanga'. Fact sheet 11 on 'The Big Yawn' Coal Mine mentions that '**Diamond is made from carbon and coal is too – but its carbon atoms are arranged differently.**' It goes on to refer to coal as '**the most commonly used fossil fuel in Olanga**'.The fuel referred to in the first notice must, therefore, be coal. So coal is sometimes called 'Black Diamond', and there is a lump of coal on the lab top! A dead end here.

Pages 80 & 81

The last time you saw Mr. Percy Smart, manager of *Snoots & Co Bank*, he was in this photograph in the file at Gertrude Rook's office on pages 62 & 63. He was bound and gagged and described as being an unidentified kidnap victim of SNATCH. Perhaps they forced him to work for them? It's not the sort of question you can ask him really . . .

Pages 82 & 83

The so-called 'Black Diamond' in the photograph looks just like the crystal paperweight on the desk in the acting assistant deputy curator's office on pages 54 & 55. There is a similar paperweight – though covered in dust – in Gertrude Rook's office on pages 60 & 61. Surely this can't really be the real *Black Diamond*? In one of the newspaper clippings on pages 50 & 51, it is stated that 'Though extremely rich, Count Lukki was in the habit of giving his friends the same gift every year: a cut-glass paperweight.'

Pages 84 & 85

Archie Rook has left his wife Gertrude a list of what he plans to do today, but pinned it to the wall the wrong way around. You can, however, still see the writing through the paper. If you look at the time (4:25pm) and read the back-to-front letters, you'll see the entry: '*Some time between 4 o'clock and 5 o'clock, I plan to do some window shopping at Jake's Jewels 'n' Gems.*' That's where he should be. It's a shop about twenty-five minutes from the Rooks' house.

Did you also spot that the cut-in-half red and silver can containing gems is just like the one on the SNATCH members' card table in Room 202 of the Hotel New Amsterdam (on pages 68 & 69), and like the crushed can in the site office at the Black Eagle Diamond Mine on pages 72 & 73. Archie Rook must be involved in diamond smuggling with SNATCH!

Pages 86 & 87

Sid Nasty, leader of SNATCH. The object is the black dagger, studded with gems, sticking out from under a tray of rings. You've seen it before in black and white. In the photo of Nasty in the file on pages 62 & 63, he's cleaning his nails with it. Nasty may be the mastermind behind the world's most successful jewel thefts but - as his profile says - he '**will steal gems wherever and whenever possible**'.

Pages 88 & 89

So you want to know who stole the *Black Diamond*? Well, you won't find the answer on this page. This is your one last chance to make up your mind who *you* think did it. Remember all those points in "**An important reminder to the reader**". Ready? Then turn the page and hold it up against a mirror . . .

THE SOLUTION

Count Lukki is described as a 'philatelist' as well as a gem collector in a newspaper clipping on page 50. As the dictionary definition on page 51 explains, a philatelist is someone who collects stamps.

In the paperwork in the manager's office at Snoots & Co Bank, on pages 82 & 83, you learn that the package said to include the Black Diamond was sent by courier. The package was put in the hands of Herbert 'Swifty' Morris who, in turn, went from Olanga to New York to hand it directly to Count Lukki in person. Why, then, was there a stamp on the box when – in the paperwork on pages 82 & 83 – it clearly states 'hand-to-hand delivery, no stamp required'?

In Count Lukki's instructions in his will, quoted by Gertrude Sparrow in a newspaper clipping on page 51, it states that Thackery was to be sent the Black Diamond 'along with the original packaging with which he, the Count, first received it from Olanga.' It goes on to say that 'Thackery was an expert and that he would realize the Black Diamond's great value' when he saw it. Notice Lukki was careful to avoid saying that he received the Black Diamond in the package . . . which could suggest that it was never in it, but if not *in* it, where? On it, perhaps?

A number of stamps have appeared throughout the mission. Some of those in the album donated to the Earl E. Byrdd Institute by Lukki, on pages 52 & 53, have a similar diamond-shaped design in the middle to those in Captain Appul's drawer at Verstroodl Police H.Q. on pages 74 & 75. They are, in fact, Olangan stamps . . . But there was only one black Olangan stamp with the diamond motif, and that was stuck to the original package. You can see it in the acting assistant deputy curator's office on pages 54 & 55.

In fact, the Olangan Black Diamond is not a precious gem at all. It is one of the rarest stamps in history – known only to a handful of the most expert of expert stamp collectors. No wonder everyone, including Sid Nasty and SNATCH thought it must be a real diamond! Count Lukki was always worried about thieves, so decided to use a trick. He arranged for a worthless paperweight to be put inside the package, and the $2.5m Black Diamond stamp to be stuck on the outside. A thief would never realize that the stamp itself was the prize!

But Lukki knew that Thackery would know what it was and how valuable it was – he said as much in a newspaper article. But, when Lukki died and the institute inherited the package, Thackery claimed that the Black Diamond was missing. In fact, he even went along with pretending that he thought it was a real diamond. That was because Thackery planned to remove the Black Diamond from the package, once the fuss had died down. His wife has expensive tastes for jewels and he'd arranged to sell the stamp in secret to buy more for her.

If that's not proof enough, think back to Thackery's office when he was called away to speak to someone named Olive. If you use the same code as used by the institute to denote who donated what, you'll find OLIVE comes out as LOREV. This is the name of the top dealer in stolen goods mentioned in Gertrude Rook's file on Spikey Muffin.

It was Thackery who stole the Black Diamond. Did you catch him?

WHERE IS THE PIRATE'S TREASURE?

Your mission is to find Captain Blackeye's lost treasure by following the clues throughout the adventure. But beware! You are about to enter a world of pirates, buried treasure, dastardly deeds and double-crosses. You're not the only one looking for the treasure. Don't trust *anybody*.

You'll play two different parts in this adventure. First, that of a navy spy in the 1780s, paid to keep a close eye on pirates terrorizing the seas. Then, *when the action moves forward over 200 years*, you will be one of a team of marine archeologists trying to track down the missing treasure today.

On every double page there are questions that need answering. These will guide you in the right direction, but you will have to use your own powers of observation and deduction to solve this baffling mystery. All the vital clues are to be found in the following pages.

Good luck shipmates!

There are helpful hints on page 138 and the answers are on pages 139 to 143. The solution to the whole mystery is on page 144.

REWARD

for creating this tale of EXCITEMENT and WONDER should go to the following LADIES & GENTLEMEN:

The Writer, Rupert Heath
The Photographer, Sue Atkinson
The Designer, Becky Halverson
The Editor, Phil Roxbee Cox

With thanks and PLENTEOUS PRAISE to all the models and model makers who made this dramatic work POSSIBLE

Not forgetting The STUPENDOUS Series Editor Ms Gaby Waters, of LONDON, England

A VISIT TO THE TAVERN

Time: Saturday, 7:17pm, 23rd July 1785
Place: The Sunny Schooner Tavern, Espinola City

As an undercover agent for the Espinolan Navy, you are reading the orders for your latest top secret mission. They were given to you by the landlord of this dockside tavern. Sipping your tropical fruit punch, you try to figure out the meaning of the song in your orders.

According to the song, where will Blackeye never go?

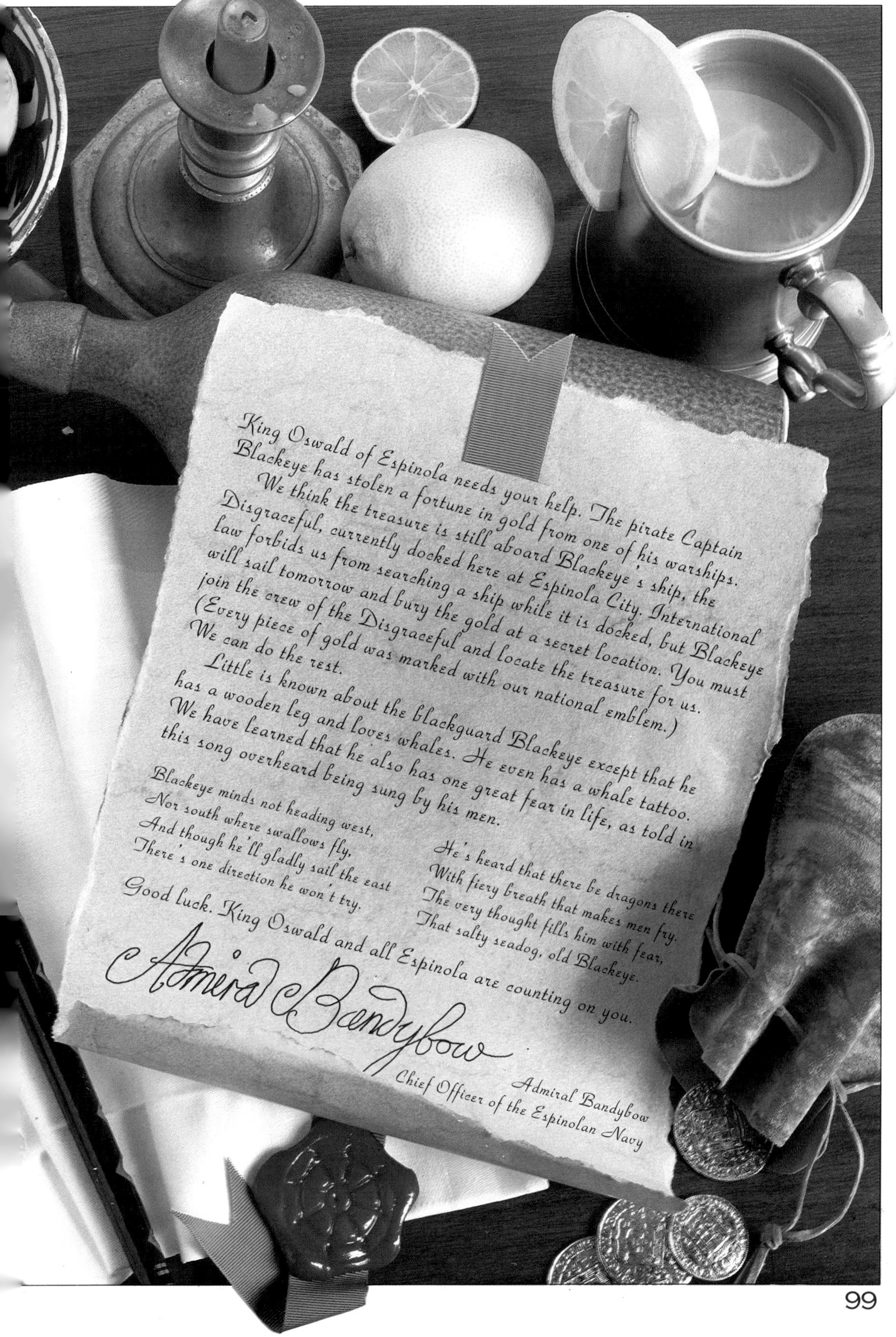
King Oswald of Espinola needs your help. The pirate Captain
Blackeye has stolen a fortune in gold from one of his warships.
We think the treasure is still aboard Blackeye's ship, the
Disgraceful, currently docked here at Espinola City. International
law forbids us from searching a ship while it is docked, but Blackeye
will sail tomorrow and bury the gold at a secret location. You must
join the crew of the Disgraceful and locate the treasure for us.
(Every piece of gold was marked with our national emblem.)
We can do the rest.
Little is known about the blackguard Blackeye except that he
has a wooden leg and loves whales. He even has a whale tattoo.
We have learned that he also has one great fear in life, as told in
this song overheard being sung by his men.
Blackeye minds not heading west,
Nor south where swallows fly,
And though he'll gladly sail the east
There's one direction he won't try.
He's heard that there be dragons there
With fiery breath that makes men fry.
The very thought fills him with fear,
That salty seadog, old Blackeye.
Good luck. King Oswald and all Espinola are counting on you.
Admiral Bandybow
Admiral Bandybow
Chief Officer of the Espinolan Navy

Crew's Duties, 26th July
Any sailor found shirking will be made to walk the plank.
10am-10.30am Hornpipe dancing
10.30am-11.30am Ginty Widdershin's poetry class in Captain's cabin
11.30am-1.00pm Cut-throat Kevin & Crowsnest Collins: paint cannons red and yellow using special paint
12 midday-1.30pm Scurvy McBurns, Powder Monkey and Samuel 'Shanty' Splicer: swab poop deck.
4.30pm-6pm Powder Monkey's sail-sewing class on foredeck
6pm-8pm Mainbrace splicing for all
9pm Bed
All loose personal items to be removed when working on deck. This avoids damaging the wood and enraging the captain.

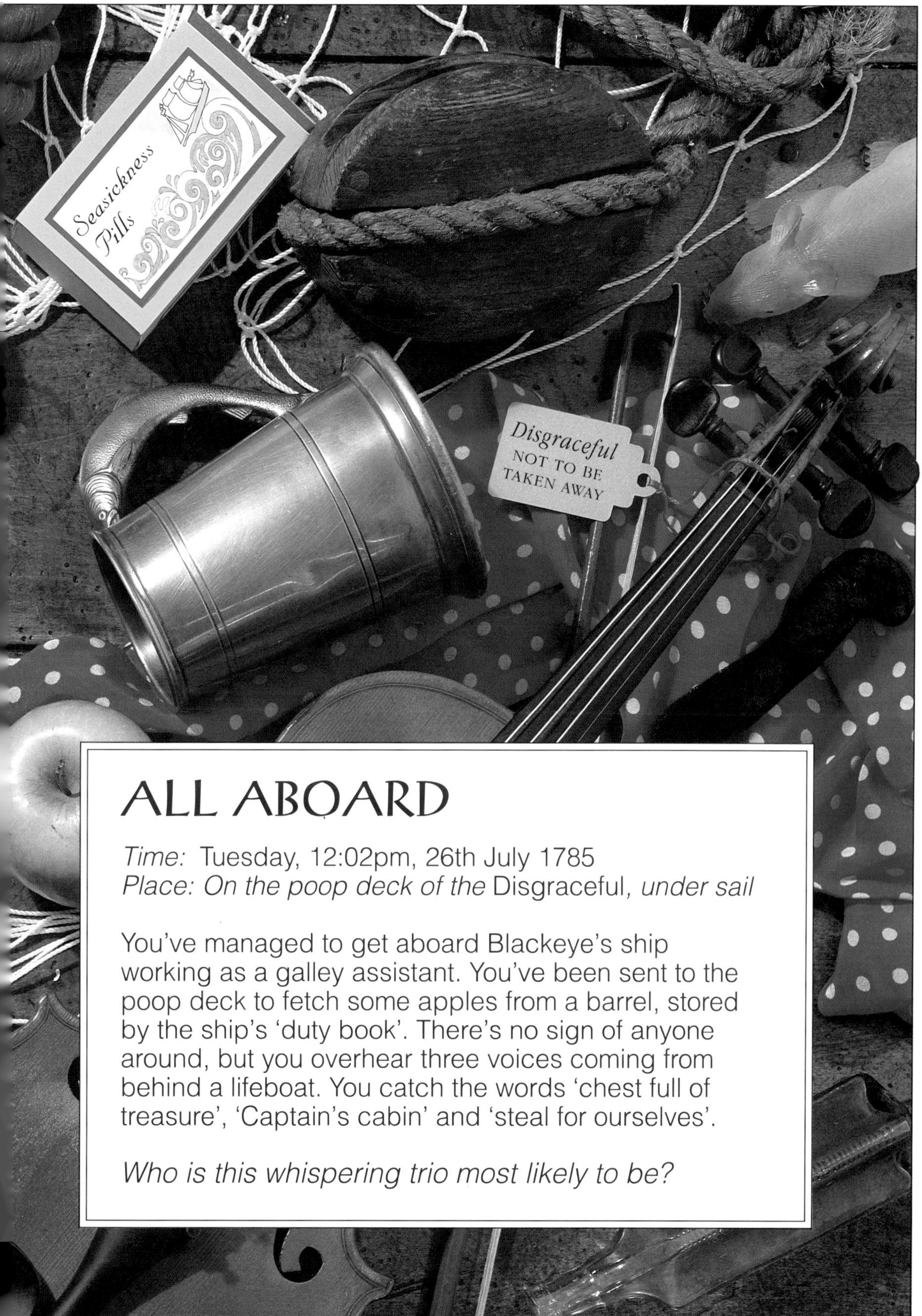
Seasickness
Pills
Disgraceful
NOT TO BE
TAKEN AWAY

ALL ABOARD

Time: Tuesday, 12:02pm, 26th July 1785
Place: On the poop deck of the Disgraceful*, under sail*

You've managed to get aboard Blackeye's ship working as a galley assistant. You've been sent to the poop deck to fetch some apples from a barrel, stored by the ship's 'duty book'. There's no sign of anyone around, but you overhear three voices coming from behind a lifeboat. You catch the words 'chest full of treasure', 'Captain's cabin' and 'steal for ourselves'.

Who is this whispering trio most likely to be?

Shanty

PLOTTING AHEAD

Time: Tuesday, 12:18pm, 26th July 1785
Place: The desk in Captain Blackeye's cabin

A tornado is blowing and the cry goes out: 'Batten down the hatches, me hearties!'. You've taken the chance to slip into the captain's cabin to see what you can find. You're facing in the direction the ship is sailing. Before you is a desk with a sea chart and a compass on it.

What is strange about the direction shown on the compass?

OREGANO
ISLAND
TARRAGON
ISLAND
CINNAMON
ISLAND
ESPINOLA
CITY
RUSTICA
N
E
W
S
ESPINOLA
ANTILLIAN
OCEAN
INCENSE
ISLAND
CARDAMON
ISLAND
SAFFRON
ISLAND
NAVY SHIPS IN
THESE WATERS
SHARKS
RIVAL PIRATES IN
THESE WATERS
SEA SERPENTS
MOUSE PRINTS
OUR ROUTE
10
Scurvy

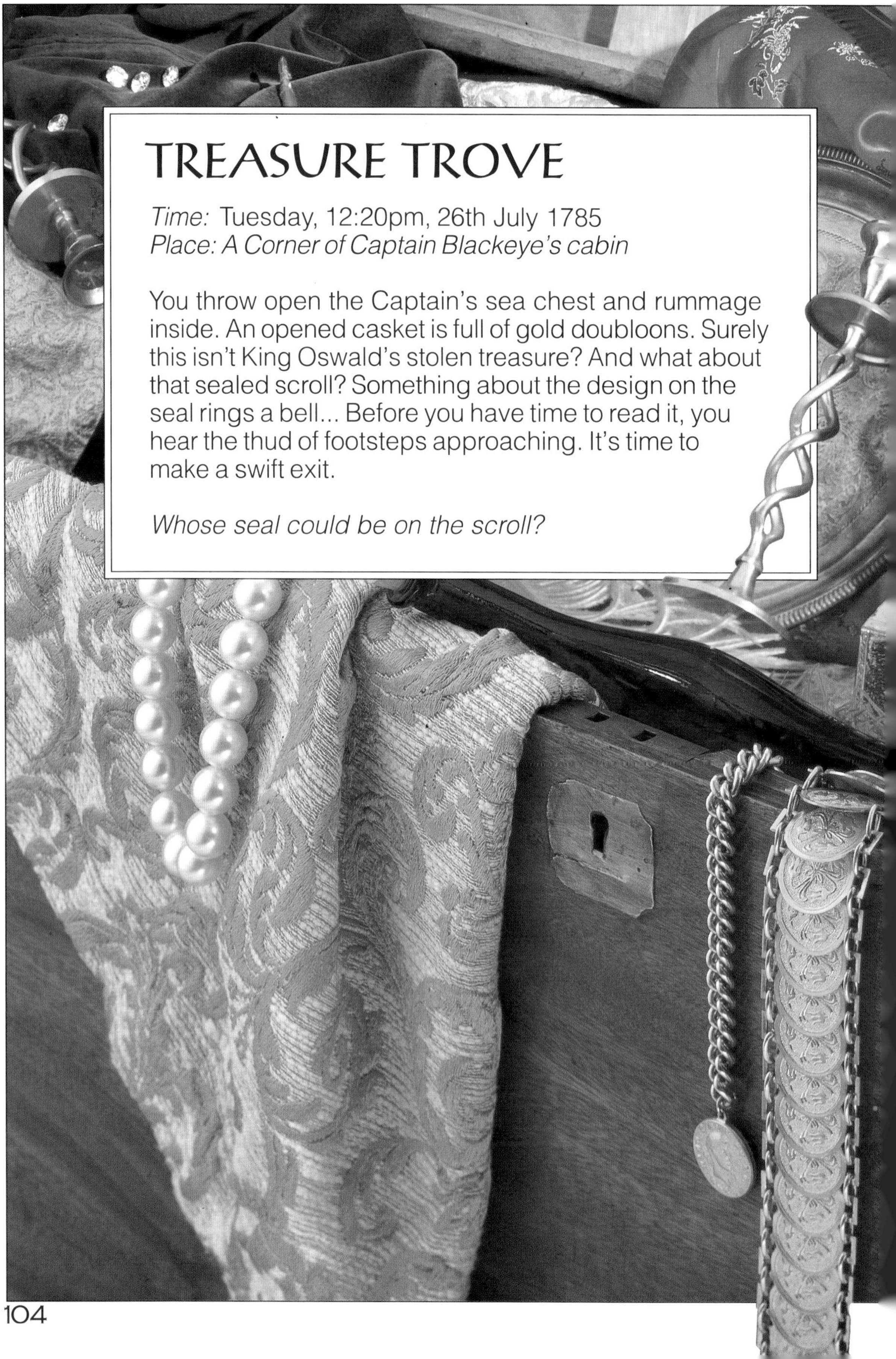

TREASURE TROVE

Time: Tuesday, 12:20pm, 26th July 1785
Place: A Corner of Captain Blackeye's cabin

You throw open the Captain's sea chest and rummage inside. An opened casket is full of gold doubloons. Surely this isn't King Oswald's stolen treasure? And what about that sealed scroll? Something about the design on the seal rings a bell... Before you have time to read it, you hear the thud of footsteps approaching. It's time to make a swift exit.

Whose seal could be on the scroll?

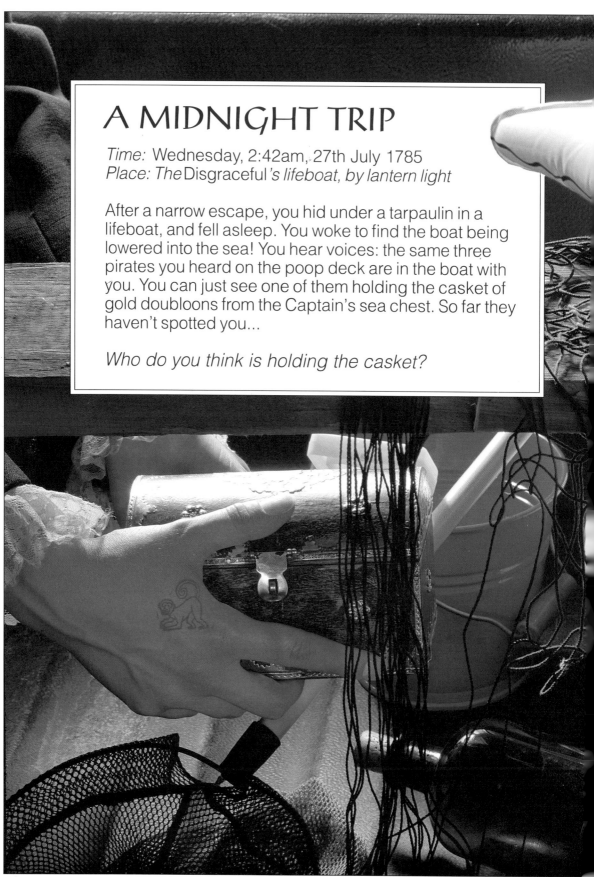

A MIDNIGHT TRIP

Time: Wednesday, 2:42am, 27th July 1785
Place: The Disgraceful*'s lifeboat, by lantern light*

After a narrow escape, you hid under a tarpaulin in a lifeboat, and fell asleep. You woke to find the boat being lowered into the sea! You hear voices: the same three pirates you heard on the poop deck are in the boat with you. You can just see one of them holding the casket of gold doubloons from the Captain's sea chest. So far they haven't spotted you...

Who do you think is holding the casket?

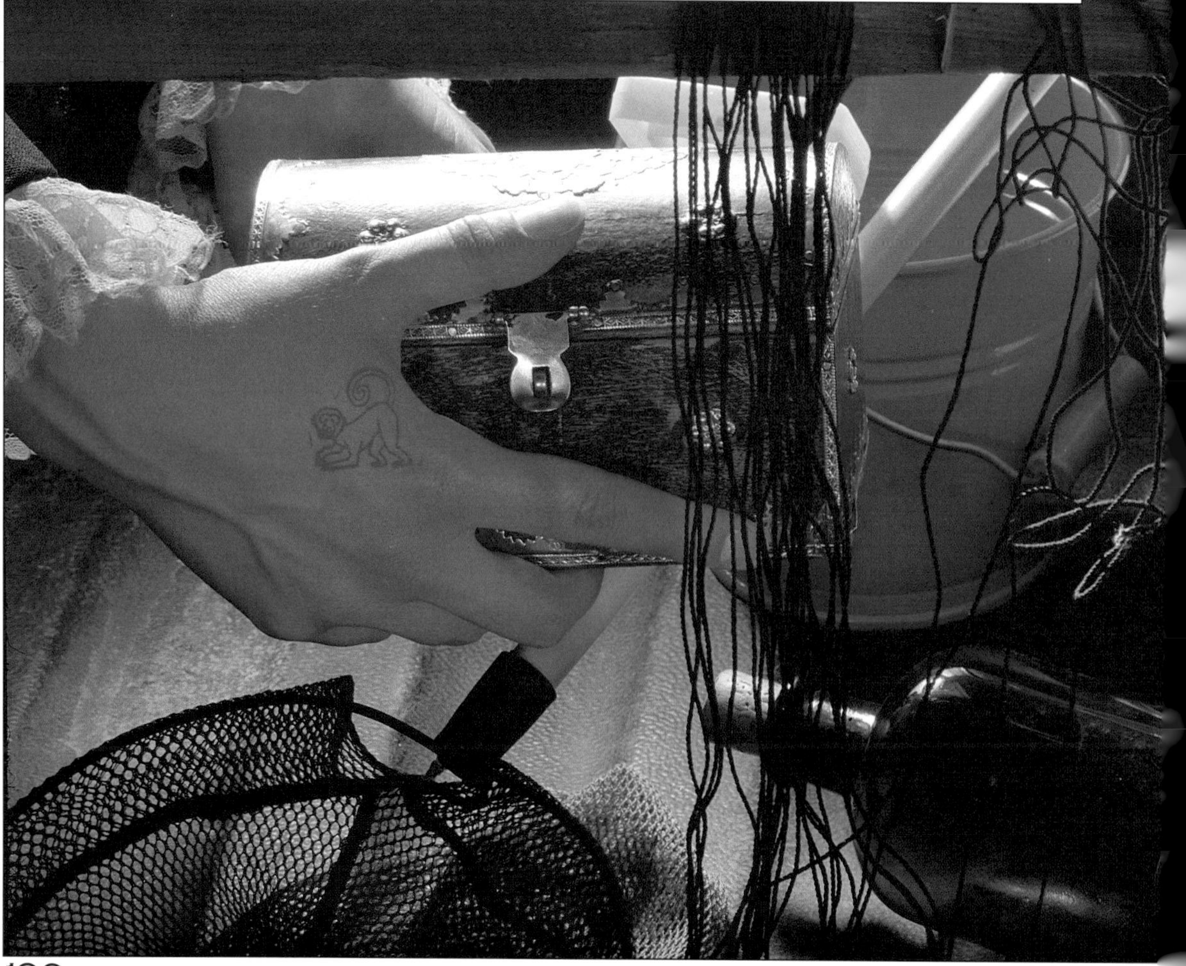

ON THE BEACH

Time: Wednesday, before dawn, 27th July 1785
Place: A desert island, bathed in blue moonlight

When the others leave the boat, you steal after them. In a fruit-filled clearing you see an 'X' marking a spot, and overhear three familiar voices. 'Stop stepping on my feet, Scurvy!' says a woman. 'I can't help where I put my feet, Powder,' replies a gruff voice. 'My shoes are too tight!' pipes up a third. You stare at the one leg you can see.

Who does the leg belong to?

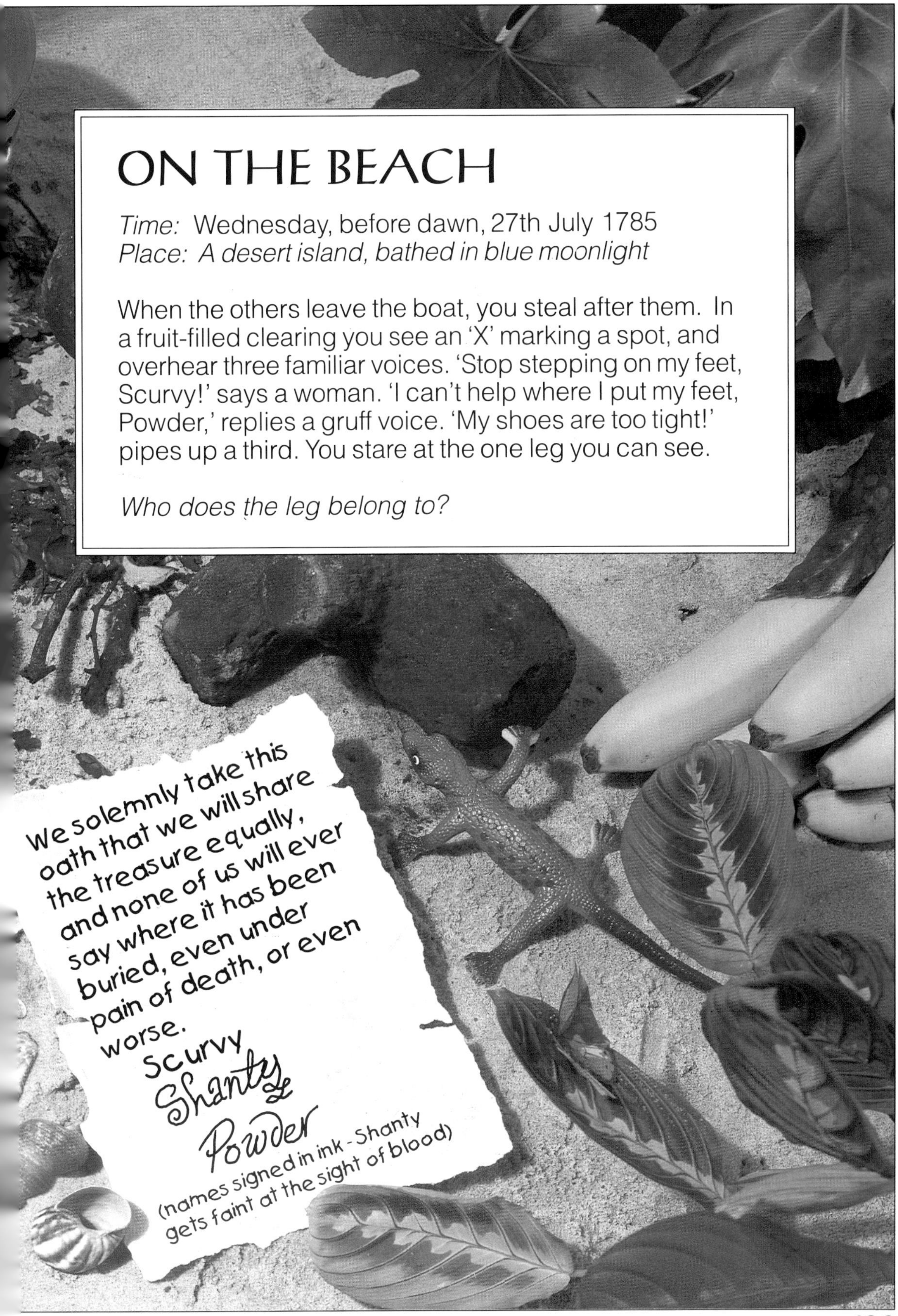
We solemnly take this oath that we will share the treasure equally, and none of us will ever say where it has been buried, even under pain of death, or even worse.
Scurvy
Shanty
Powder
(names signed in ink - Shanty gets faint at the sight of blood)

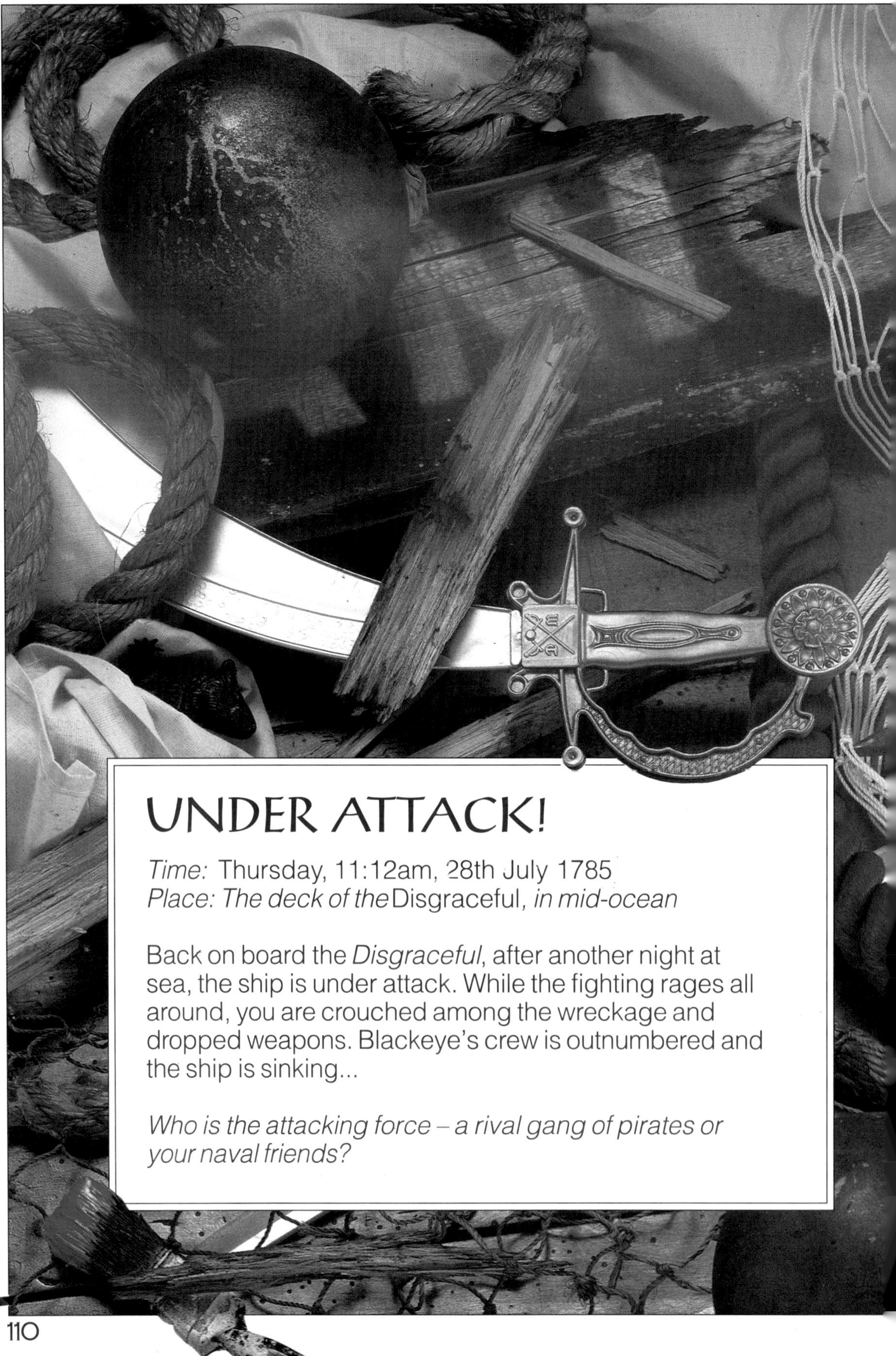

UNDER ATTACK!

Time: Thursday, 11:12am, 28th July 1785
Place: The deck of the Disgraceful, *in mid-ocean*

Back on board the *Disgraceful*, after another night at sea, the ship is under attack. While the fighting rages all around, you are crouched among the wreckage and dropped weapons. Blackeye's crew is outnumbered and the ship is sinking...

Who is the attacking force – a rival gang of pirates or your naval friends?

Gold-i-lux
Paint

Ladies' Pistol
Ship's Biscuits
Blackeye's Pistol

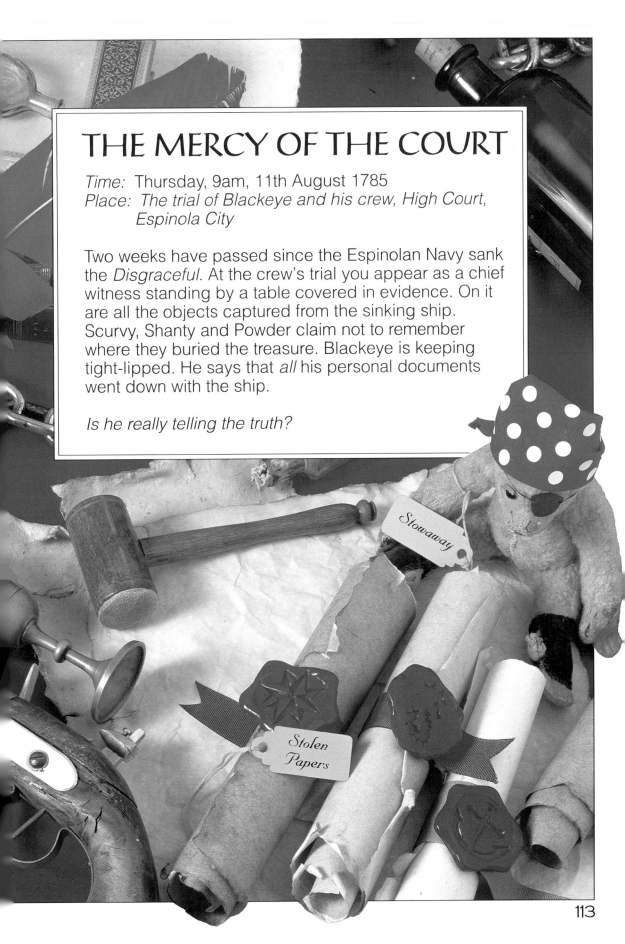

THE MERCY OF THE COURT

Time: Thursday, 9am, 11th August 1785
Place: The trial of Blackeye and his crew, High Court, Espinola City

Two weeks have passed since the Espinolan Navy sank the *Disgraceful*. At the crew's trial you appear as a chief witness standing by a table covered in evidence. On it are all the objects captured from the sinking ship. Scurvy, Shanty and Powder claim not to remember where they buried the treasure. Blackeye is keeping tight-lipped. He says that *all* his personal documents went down with the ship.

Is he really telling the truth?

Stowaway
Stolen Papers

Fondant creams are 'root of all evil' says Minister for Law & Order
Fondant creams have been banned from Espinola following a report published by the new Minister for Law & Order, Mr. Joshua 'Iron Fist' Crosspatch.
'I believe that fondant creams are responsible for all the problems in Espinola, so I've made them illegal,' he told reporters at a press conference on Wednesday. Anyone found in possession of fondant creams is liable ... in prison. Smuggling of ...
Captain Blackeye.
Notorious for stealing King Oswald's treasure.
- 25 -
of the most ruthless buccaneers ever to the seven seas, Captain Barnabas Blackeye today most famous for his daring theft of King Oswald of Espinola's treasure in 1785.
A man of many talents, Captain Blackeye is credited as having 'one of ye finest beards of his generation', as having invented a very early form of photography and as having 'a most beauteous and thin ankle for such a large man'.
No one knows how Blackeye managed to steal King Oswald's precious gold, and no one knows what became of it.
Some believe that the treasure was later stolen from Blackeye by members of his own rag bag crew.
Following the destruction of Blackeye's ship, the Disgraceful, on 28 July 1785, three crew members (Splicer, McBurns and Monkey) claimed to have stolen Blackeye's gold but said that they couldn't remember where they'd buried it.
Another theory is that King Oswald's stolen treasure was melted down, made into one large object and painted over to disguise its true value. The treasure is believed to be worth worth over $5m today.
- 26 -
Pirate's possessions presented to pub
from our own correspondent
A sea chest belonging to the most notorious of all Espinolan pirates, Captain Blackeye, is to be kept in the old sea dog's best-loved watering hole, the Sunny Schooner Tavern.
In 1785, the chest was washed up on shore and kept by a local fisherman, Juan Mullett after Blackeye's ship, the Disgraceful, was sunk in battle.
A direct descendant of Mr. Mullet presented the chest to the Espinolan government in 1893 and, since then, it has been kept in storage, with the few other items salvaged from the Disgraceful including the ship's
irate treasure map found in l
from our life & limb correspondent
A rolled-up map, believed to show the location of pi gold worth $5m, has been found in a wooden leg at Espinola Maritime Museum. The leg, which belonged Captain Blackeye, has been in the museum for 150 yea
'When the leg was taken for cleaning, the map simp fell to the floor,' said the curator of limbs, Alfred Elbo The map is believed to show a number of island location where King Oswald's stolen treasure could be hidden.
'The treasure is part of Espinola's history, and we ar determined to claim it back for our country,' said Directo of Underwater Operations, Dr. John Greygoose. 'We start by exploring the area where we believe th Disgraceful sank. After that, we'll explore the islands marked on the map. These are excitin

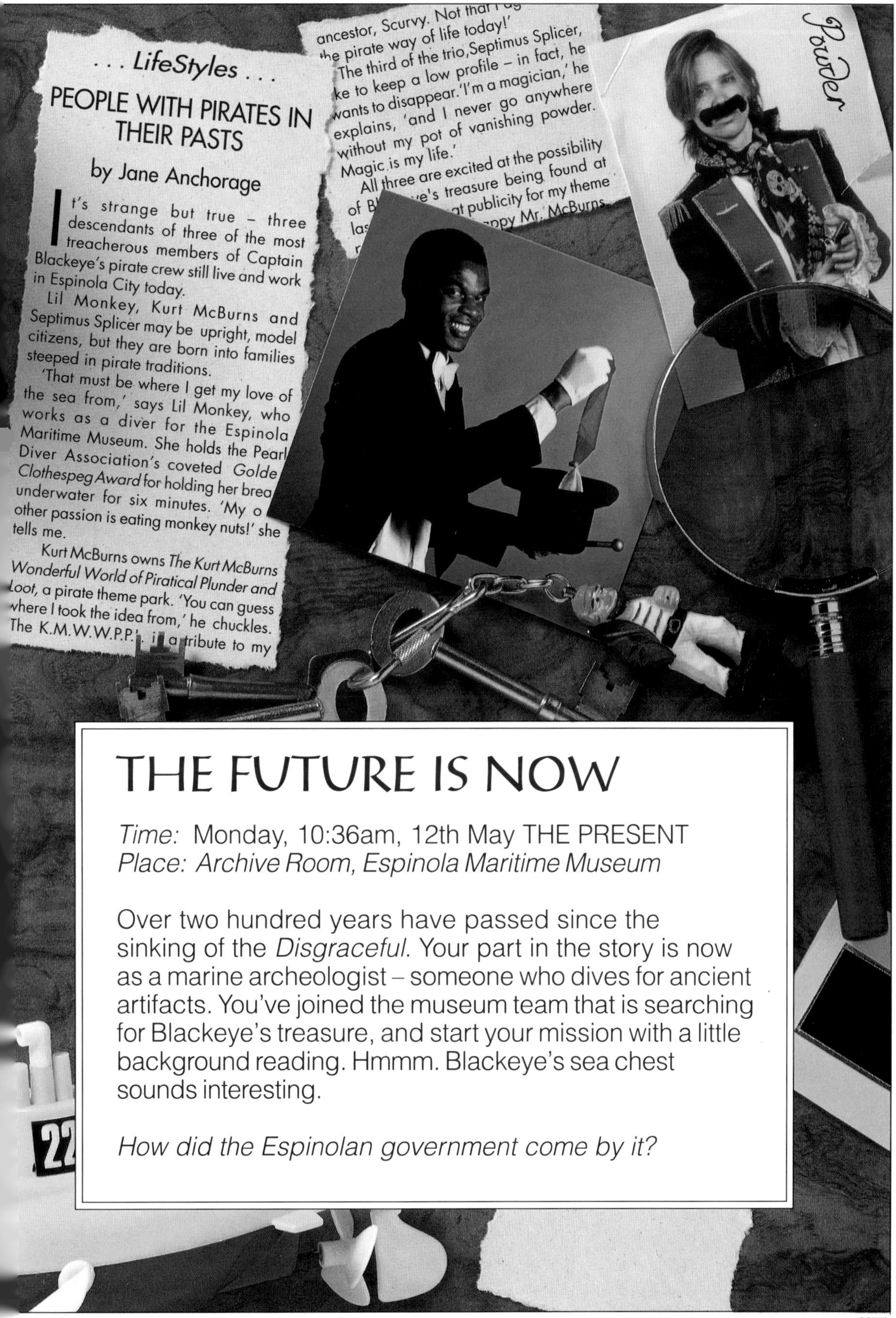
. . . LifeStyles . . .
PEOPLE WITH PIRATES IN THEIR PASTS
by Jane Anchorage
It's strange but true – three descendants of three of the most treacherous members of Captain Blackeye's pirate crew still live and work in Espinola City today.
Lil Monkey, Kurt McBurns and Septimus Splicer may be upright, model citizens, but they are born into families steeped in pirate traditions.
'That must be where I get my love of the sea from,' says Lil Monkey, who works as a diver for the Espinola Maritime Museum. She holds the Pearl Diver Association's coveted Golde Clothespeg Award for holding her brea underwater for six minutes. 'My o other passion is eating monkey nuts!' she tells me.
Kurt McBurns owns The Kurt McBurns Wonderful World of Piratical Plunder and Loot, a pirate theme park. 'You can guess where I took the idea from,' he chuckles. The K.M.W.W.P.P.L. is a tribute to my
ancestor, Scurvy. Not that I ag the pirate way of life today!'
The third of the trio, Septimus Splicer, ke to keep a low profile – in fact, he wants to disappear. 'I'm a magician,' he explains, 'and I never go anywhere without my pot of vanishing powder. Magic is my life.'
All three are excited at the possibility of Bl ve's treasure being found at las at publicity for my theme ppy Mr. McBurns.
Powder
22

THE FUTURE IS NOW

Time: Monday, 10:36am, 12th May THE PRESENT
Place: Archive Room, Espinola Maritime Museum

Over two hundred years have passed since the sinking of the *Disgraceful*. Your part in the story is now as a marine archeologist – someone who dives for ancient artifacts. You've joined the museum team that is searching for Blackeye's treasure, and start your mission with a little background reading. Hmmm. Blackeye's sea chest sounds interesting.

How did the Espinolan government come by it?

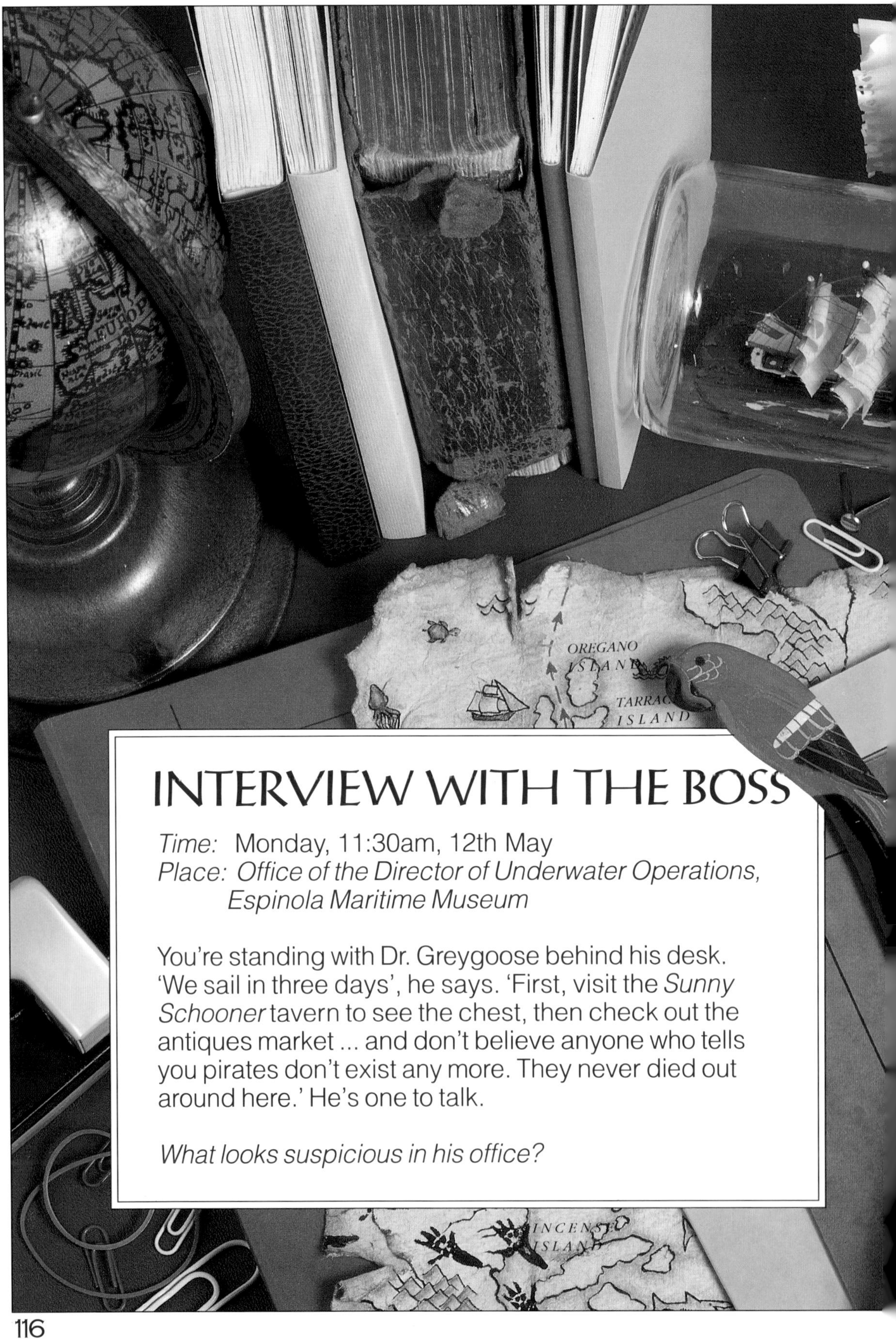
OREGANO

INTERVIEW WITH THE BOSS

Time: Monday, 11:30am, 12th May
Place: Office of the Director of Underwater Operations, Espinola Maritime Museum

You're standing with Dr. Greygoose behind his desk. 'We sail in three days', he says. 'First, visit the *Sunny Schooner* tavern to see the chest, then check out the antiques market ... and don't believe anyone who tells you pirates don't exist any more. They never died out around here.' He's one to talk.

What looks suspicious in his office?

FONDA CREAM
TREASURE TROVE MONTHLY
"FIND OF THE MONTH"
Dr. John Greygoose and Lil Monkey proudly display their latest archeological find. Lil will be accompanying Dr. Greygoose on the mission to recover King Oswald's treasure.

Antiques Market

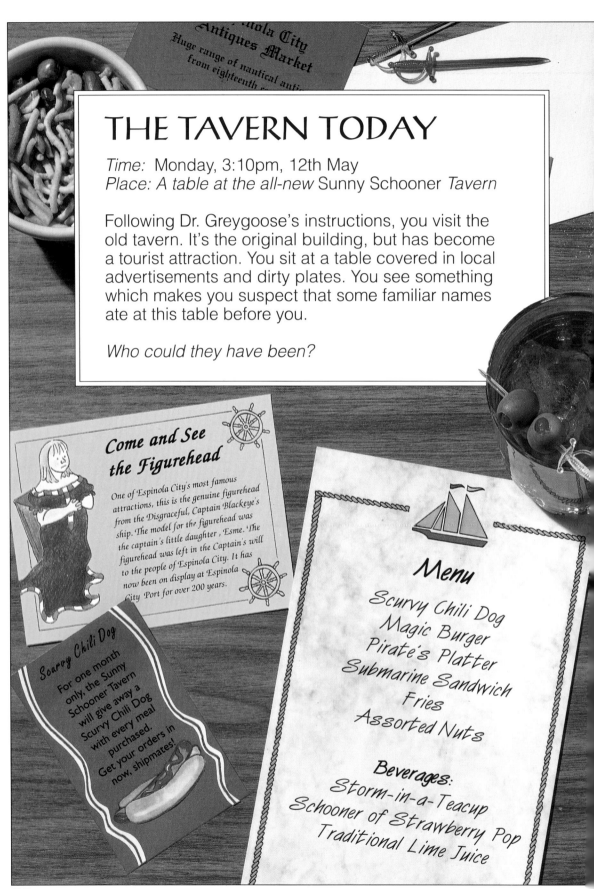

THE TAVERN TODAY

Time: Monday, 3:10pm, 12th May
Place: A table at the all-new Sunny Schooner *Tavern*

Following Dr. Greygoose's instructions, you visit the old tavern. It's the original building, but has become a tourist attraction. You sit at a table covered in local advertisements and dirty plates. You see something which makes you suspect that some familiar names ate at this table before you.

Who could they have been?

Come and See the Figurehead
One of Espinola City's most famous attractions, this is the genuine figurehead from the Disgraceful, Captain Blackeye's ship. The model for the figurehead was the captain's little daughter, Esme. The figurehead was left in the Captain's will to the people of Espinola City. It has now been on display at Espinola City Port for over 200 years.
Scurvy Chili Dog
For one month only, the Sunny Schooner Tavern will give away a Scurvy Chili Dog with every meal purchased. Get your orders in now, shipmates!
Menu
Scurvy Chili Dog
Magic Burger
Pirate's Platter
Submarine Sandwich
Fries
Assorted Nuts
Beverages:
Storm-in-a-Teacup
Schooner of Strawberry Pop
Traditional Lime Juice

A hearty welcome is guaranteed at:
The Kurt McBurns
Wonderful World of Piratical Plunder and Loot
The most authentic and amazing Pirate theme park in the world
See you there!
FOOD ORDER
S
2 SC Dogs 3.40
1 M Burger 3.60
1 M Nuts 1.95
Beverages – NIL
TOTAL 8.95
Gold-i-lux Paint
Manufactured in Espinola for over 250 years, this paint is formulated specially to cover 24 carat gold. Guaranteed all-weather protection, no chipping or flaking.
Tried the rest? Buy the best!

Rfad this riddlf if yf bf
Bold fnough to stfal from mf.
Rfmfmbfr now what you arf told:
All that glittfrs is not gold.
If yf wish your coursf sft fair
Look for thf maidfn with goldfn hair.
fool's gold yf will find,
truf trfasurf yf
lfavf bfhind.

THE OLD SEA CHEST

Time: Monday, 3:30pm, 12th May
Place: The attic of the Sunny Schooner *Tavern*

The landlord has been expecting you. He leads you up to the attic, where Captain Blackeye's old sea chest is now stored. It is full of items salvaged from the wreck of the *Disgraceful*. The objects are still bright and gleaming after over 200 years. Leaving Blackeye's logbook for later, you eagerly unroll the torn scroll. On it is a coded message.

Can you decipher what it says?

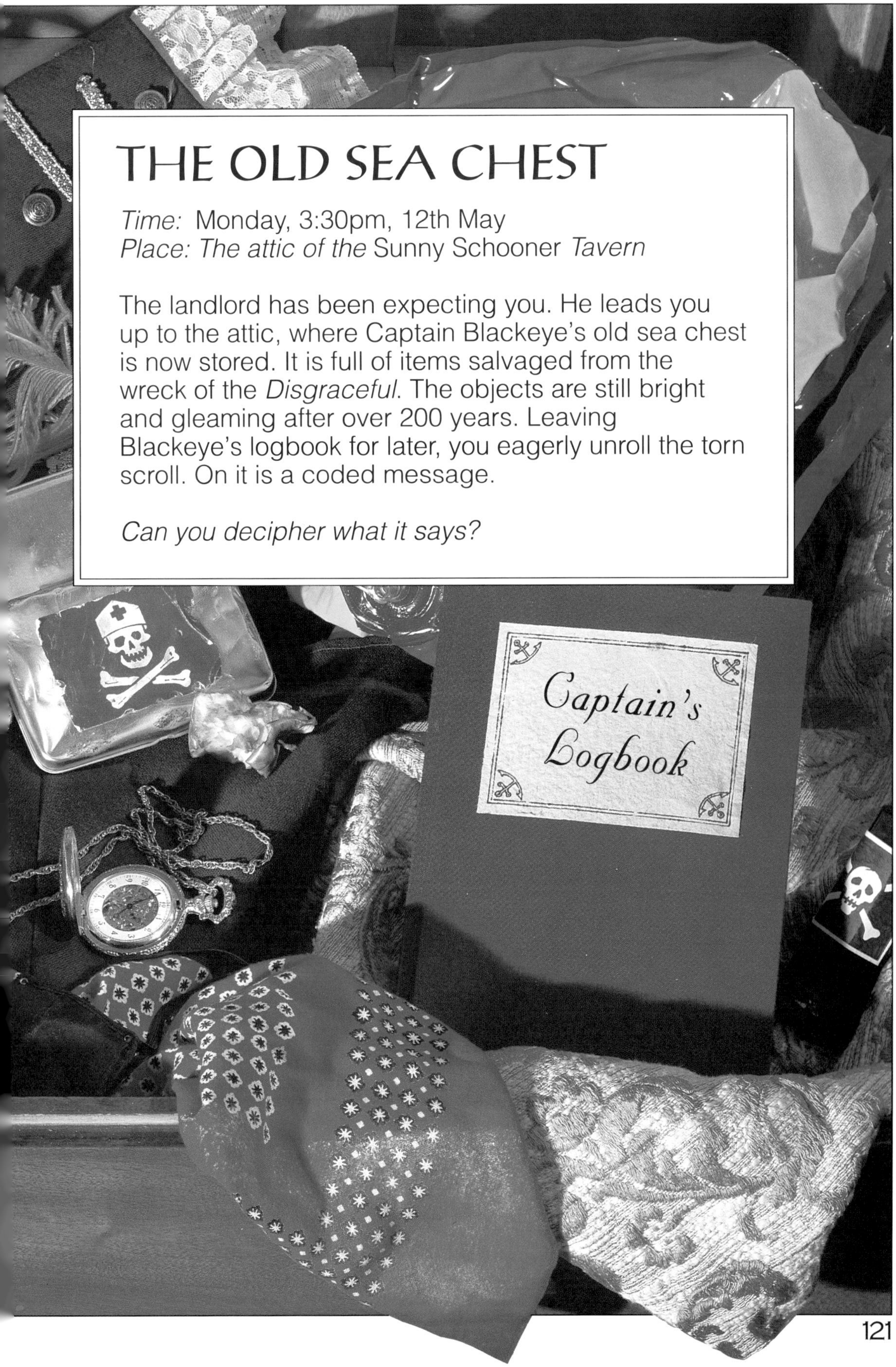
Captain's Logbook

Or flsf it's
And Oswald's
Esme

IN THE MARKET FOR CLUES

Time: Tuesday, 8:30am,13th May
Place: Mr. Anka's stall, Espinola City Antiques Market

On Dr. Greygoose's advice, you start the day with a visit to an antiques dealer. He is trying to interest you in an old model ship. At least it looks more valuable than that furry parrot. Still, you have seen two things which could prove important.

What are they?

Examples of pirate gold, melted down and remade into other objects

A MYSTERIOUS MEETING

Time: Thursday, 7am, 15th May
Place: At the port, Espinola City

Today is the day you set off in search of King Oswald's stolen treasure. You decide to stroll around the dock before boarding Dr. Greygoose's ship, the *Aspidistra*. You see him deep in conversation with a man, half-hidden by a basket of fruit. One glimpse of you and they both hurry away.

Any clues to the stranger's identity?
Anything suspicious left behind?

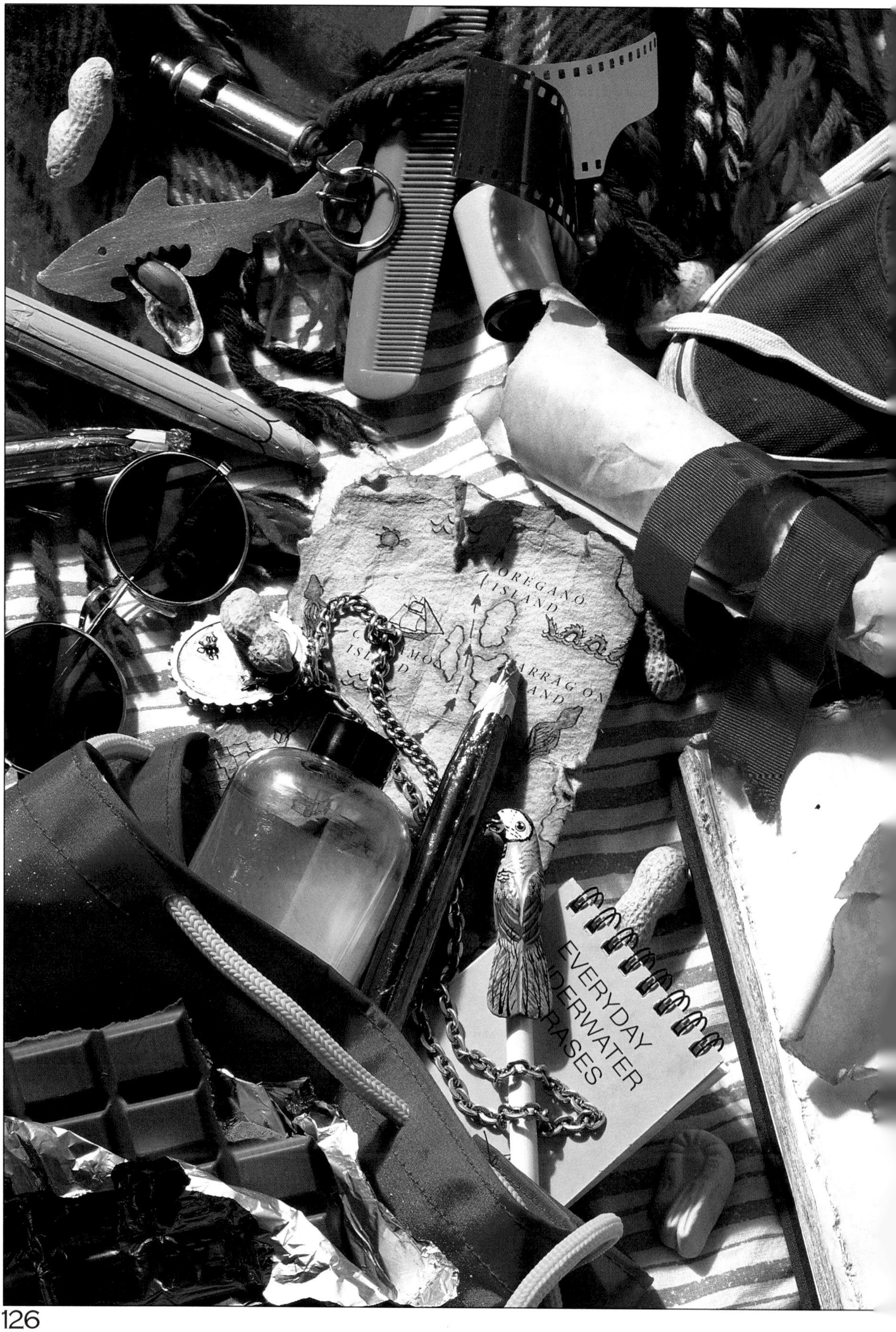
OREGANO ISLAND
EVERYDAY

FULL STEAM AHEAD

Time: Thursday, 9:51am, 15th May
Place: In a cabin, aboard the Aspidistra

The search has begun for the sunken wreck of the *Disgraceful*. It's going to be a rough voyage. Even the ship's parrot has turned a little green. You're in a cabin full of crew members' belongings, looking at Blackeye's logbook. After what you've seen, you're suspicious of spies, and something suggests the descendant of Samuel 'Shanty' Splicer is on board!

What is it?

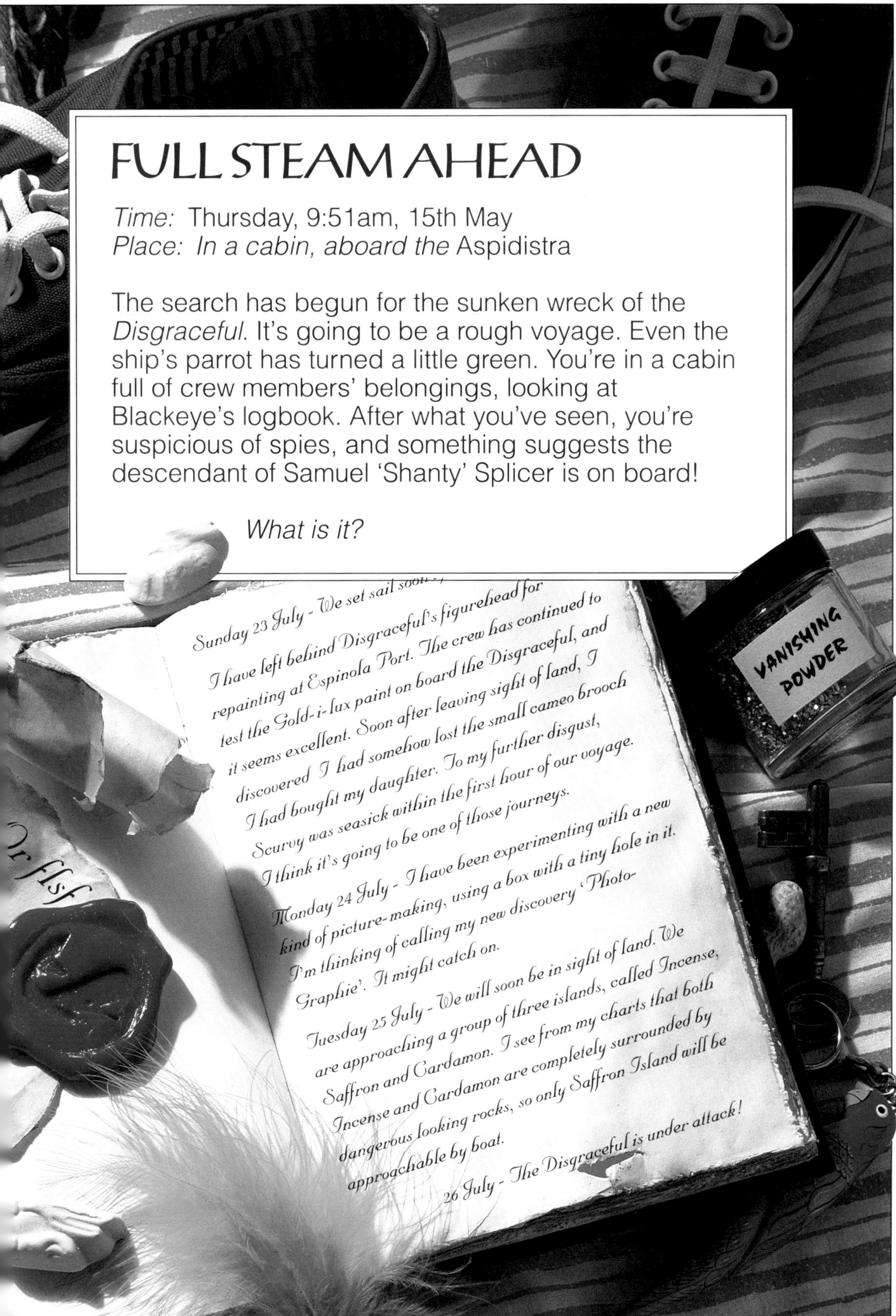
Sunday 23 July - We set sail soon
I have left behind Disgraceful's figurehead for
repainting at Espinola Port. The crew has continued to
test the Gold-i-lux paint on board the Disgraceful, and
it seems excellent. Soon after leaving sight of land, I
discovered I had somehow lost the small cameo brooch
I had bought my daughter. To my further disgust,
Scurvy was seasick within the first hour of our voyage.
I think it's going to be one of those journeys.
Monday 24 July - I have been experimenting with a new
kind of picture-making, using a box with a tiny hole in it.
I'm thinking of calling my new discovery 'Photo-
Graphie'. It might catch on.
Tuesday 25 July - We will soon be in sight of land. We
are approaching a group of three islands, called Incense,
Saffron and Cardamon. I see from my charts that both
Incense and Cardamon are completely surrounded by
dangerous looking rocks, so only Saffron Island will be
approachable by boat.
26 July - The Disgraceful is under attack!
VANISHING POWDER

GOING DEEP

Time: Thursday, 2pm, 22nd May
Place: A speedboat, off the side of the Aspidistra

You are anchored at the spot where the *Disgraceful* was believed to have sunk. Everyone is in scuba diving gear, ready to dive, when by chance you re-check the oxygen tanks, and discover they are empty. Someone has tampered with the tanks. Surely none of your fellow divers can be suspects, as they too would have drowned.

Or would they?

GROG
Made in Rustica
Bears Rustican
national emblem

CATCH OF THE DAY

Time: Thursday, 4:09pm, 22nd May
Place: On the deck of the Aspidistra

The oxygen tanks have been refilled, the first dive has been made, and the haul is spread out on the deck. Nothing here that looks particularly valuable. If only you could be sure that these objects are from the wreck of the *Disgraceful*.

Any clues?

PIRATES
SQUALLS
SAILORS
ADRIFT
LAND AHOY
ON BOARD
BEWARE
AT ANCHOR
SHARKS
AGROUND
MORSE CODE MESSAGE NO. 1
•– – / • • • • / • – / – /
– – • / – – – / • / • • • /
– – • • / – – • • / • • – /
– • • • / – – • • / – – • • /
• • – / – • • •
A •–
B –•••
C –•–•
D –••
E •
F ••–•
G ––•
H ••••
I ••
J •–––
K –•–
L •–••
M ––
N –•
O –––
P •––•
Q ––•–
R
S
T
U
Greetings from Espinola

ESPINOLA CALLING

Time: Friday, 11am, 23rd May
Place: Radio Room on board the Aspidistra

You are told by one of the crew that there is a message for you in the Radio Room. When you arrive, there is nothing but interference on the radio. An important message has been left nonetheless.

What does the message say?

MORSE MESSAGE NO. 2
• – / – • • • / • / • / • – • /
• / • • • – / • / • – • /
• • • / • • / – • / – – •
E •
F • • – •
G – – •
H • • • •
I • •
J • – – –
K – • –
L • – • •
M – –
R • – •
S • • •
T –
U • • –
V • • • –
W • – –
X – • • –
Y – • – –
– – • •
A Postcard from Rustica

TRICKED!

Time: Friday, 11:15am, 23rd May
Place: In the hold of the Aspidistra

Passing the cargo hold, you spot an empty tea chest, a great clutter of items that have been reported missing from around the ship, and some monkey nuts – Lil Monkey's number one snack. In among the mess is a strangely worded note.

What does the note say?
Which island is likely to be the one mentioned in the note?

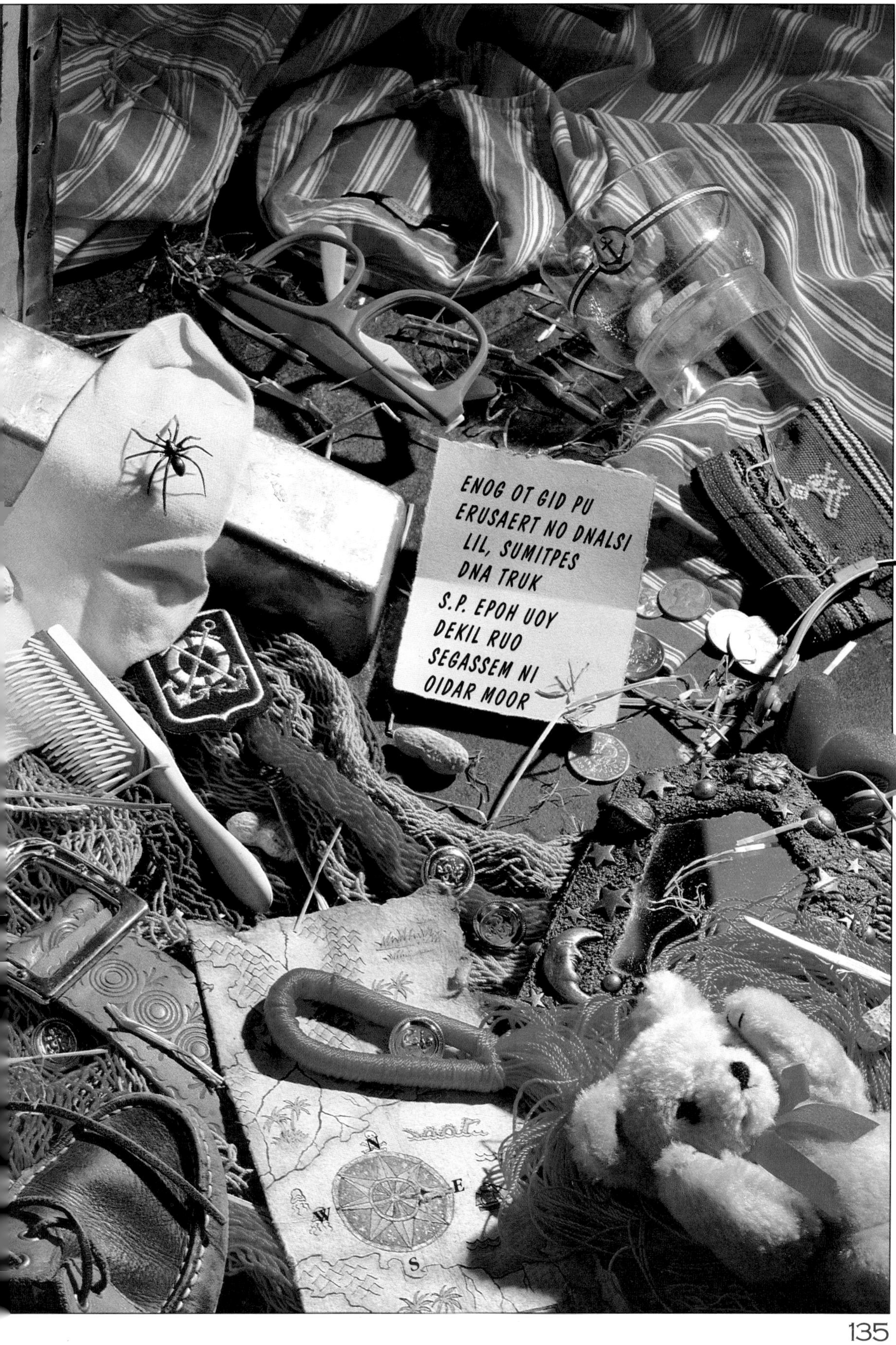

ENOG OT GID PU
ERUSAERT NO DNALSI
LIL, SUMITPES
DNA TRUK
S.P. EPOH UOY
DEKIL RUO
SEGASSEM NI
OIDAR MOOR
N
E
W
S

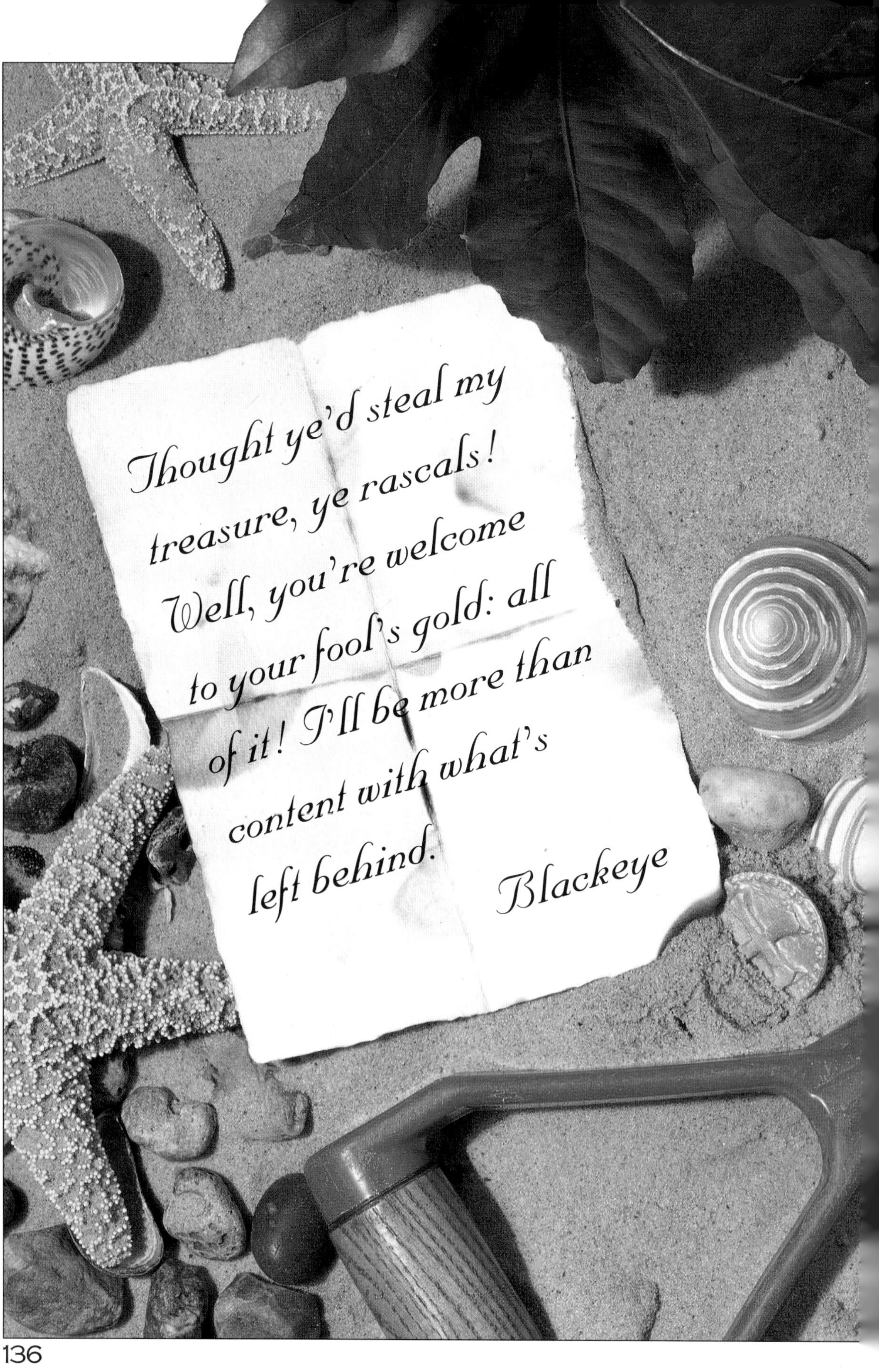
Thought ye'd steal my
treasure, ye rascals!
Well, you're welcome
to your fool's gold: all
of it! I'll be more than
content with what's
left behind.
Blackeye

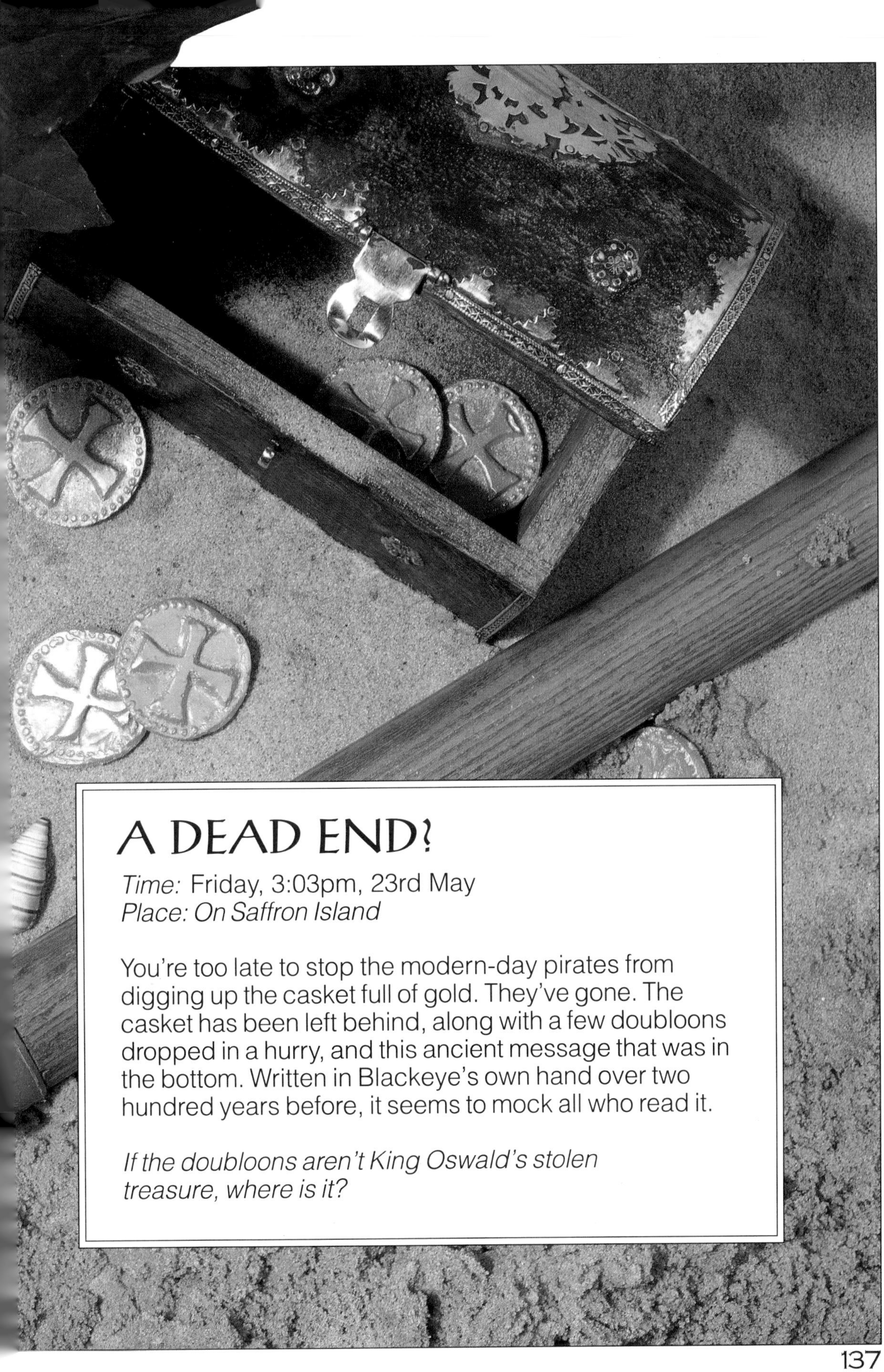

A DEAD END?

Time: Friday, 3:03pm, 23rd May
Place: On Saffron Island

You're too late to stop the modern-day pirates from digging up the casket full of gold. They've gone. The casket has been left behind, along with a few doubloons dropped in a hurry, and this ancient message that was in the bottom. Written in Blackeye's own hand over two hundred years before, it seems to mock all who read it.

If the doubloons aren't King Oswald's stolen treasure, where is it?

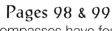

HELPFUL HINTS

Pages 98 & 99
Compasses have four points. Which one of these isn't mentioned in the song?

Pages 100 & 101
The answer could lie in the duty book. Think of time and place.

Pages 102 & 103
Look at the sea chart, study the route and don't forget that the arrow on a compass always points north.

Pages 104 & 105
There's a whale symbol on the seal. What have you already read about whales?

Pages 106 & 107
Hands sometimes hold a clue to a person's identity.

Pages 108 & 109
Legs usually come in pairs. Whose could be the exception in this adventure?

Pages 110 & 111
Study the flintlock pistols dropped in the heat of the battle.

Pages 112 & 113
Think back to Blackeye's love of whales.

Pages 114 & 115
The answer lies in one of those articles.

Pages 116 & 117
Look back at the newspaper clippings. One of the items on Dr. Greygoose's desk is very much in the news.

Pages 118 & 119
Any initial thoughts on who ate what?

Pages 120 & 121
Why are there no letter 'e's in this message? The letter 'f' appears rather too much!

Pages 122 & 123
The writing on the scrap of paper looks familiar . . . and the name 'Esme' should be familiar too.

Pages 124 & 125
Two dropped items should help you with the man's identity. As for anything else suspicious, check the fruit.

Pages 126 & 127
Septimus Splicer doesn't like being seen.

Pages 128 & 129
Oxygen lets you breathe underwater. Can you think of anyone who can hold their breath for a long time?

Pages 130 & 131
Could the initial 'C' before Collins stand for Crowsnest? Where have you come across that name before?

Pages 132 & 133
Morse Code isn't the only kind of code used on board the *Aspidistra*.

Pages 134 & 135
Think 'back-to-front'.

Pages 136 & 137
Does the answer lie in an earlier rhyme?

ANSWERS

Pages 98 & 99

The song states that there's one direction Captain Blackeye won't sail because '*He's heard that there be dragons there*'. In the first verse, it's made clear that he doesn't mind sailing west, south or east . . . so that leaves north.This must be the direction that Captain Blackeye will never go.

Pages 100 & 101

The time now is 12:02pm. According to the duty book, the only people with duties on the poop deck at the moment are Scurvy McBurns, Powder Monkey and Samuel Shanty Spicer. Apart from you, there's no one else around and the threat in the book that '*Any sailor found shirking will be made to walk the plank*' suggests that these three sailors are likely to be where they're supposed to be!

It's possible that some of the items left by the duty book belong to the whispering trio.

Pages 102 & 103

On the chart is a red dotted line which, according to the key, is 'OUR ROUTE'. If this is meant to be the course that the *Disgraceful* is now taking, then it is odd for two reasons. First, because the marked course shows us going north – a direction we know the Captain won't travel from the song on page 99. Second, although you are facing the direction in which the ship is sailing, the compass shows north to be in the opposite direction. The *Disgraceful* is, in fact, heading southward.

Pages 104 & 105

The seal on the scroll has the imprint of a whale on it. In your orders from Admiral Bandybow on page 99, you are told that the Captain loves whales and that he even has a whale tattoo – this suggests that the seal is probably Blackeye's.

Pages 106 & 107

From their voices, you know that the three pirates in the lifeboat with you now are the same three you overheard whispering on the poop deck. You suspected then that they were Scurvy McBurns, Powder Monkey and Samuel 'Shanty' Splicer. The hand holding the casket of doubloons has a small monkey tattooed on it and, of the three suspects, Powder Monkey seems the most likely candidate to have such a tattoo.

Pages 108 & 109

You know from the conversation between the three pirates from the lifeboat that they each have *two* legs – but the person in front of you has one 'real' leg and a wooden leg. The only person you know who has a wooden leg is Captain Blackeye himself (something you originally learned in your orders on page 99).

The note confirms that you were correct in identifying the three poop deck plotters.

Pages 110 & 111

It is most likely to be the Espinolan Navy. On the butt of one of the flintlock pistols – dropped on the deck in the heat of the battle – is a ship's wheel design. This matches the design on the seal attached to your orders (on page 99) from Admiral Bandybow of the Espinolan Navy.

Pages 112 & 113

Not surprisingly, the pirate Captain is lying. The scroll with the whale seal, sticking out of the books, looks suspiciously like the one you spotted in his sea chest before the ship went down.

Pages 114 & 115

The answer lies in the newspaper article headed 'Pirate's possessions presented to pub'. According to this, Blackeye's sea chest was washed up on shore after the sinking of the *Disgraceful* in 1785 and found by a fisherman named Mullet. In 1893, Mullet's descendant presented the chest to the Espinolan government.

22

Pages 116 & 117

You learned from an article on page 114 that the Espinolan Minister for Law & Order has banned fondant creams as the **'root of all evil'**. Anyone in possession of fondant creams is liable to go to prison . . . yet Dr. Greygoose appears to have a box of fondant creams – half hidden by his hanky – on his desk!

Pages 118 & 119

It seems that you've been sitting at a table that the descendants of Powder Monkey, Scurvy McBurns and Samuel 'Shanty' Splicer were eating at earlier. From the newspaper clipping headed 'PEOPLE WITH PIRATES IN THEIR PASTS', you know that their names are Septimus Splicer, Kurt McBurns and Lil Monkey.

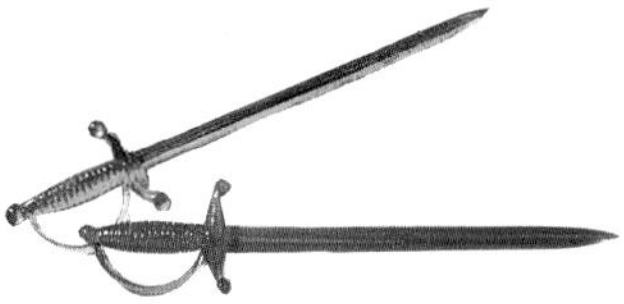

Their initials – S, K and L – match the initials written next to the food orders. (It appears that one of them was working out who-spent-what on the meal.) As if that isn't enough, the initial L appears by the order of monkey nuts – which Lil Monkey describes, in the same clipping, as being her 'other passion'.

Pages 120 & 121

The poem is in straightforward English, except for the occasional '*ye*' – which is old English for the word 'you' – and the fact that all letter 'e's have been changed to 'f's. There is also a piece missing.

Once the the 'e's have been returned to their proper places, what's left of the message reads:

Read this riddle if ye be
Bold enough to steal from me.
Remember now what you are told:
All that glitters is not gold.
If ye wish your course set fair
Look for the maiden with golden hair
. . . . gold ye will find
. . . . true treasure ye leave behind

Pages 122 & 123

The two most important items are the piece of yellowed paper and the locket. The piece of paper is the missing corner of Captain Blackeye's poem on page 120. Once the scrap has been added to the last three lines and decoded, the message ends:

Or else it's fool's gold ye will find
And Oswald's true treasure ye leave behind.

The locket could well have belonged to Captain Blackeye himself. According to an advertisement about the *Disgraceful*'s figurehead on page 118, he is said to have had a daughter called Esme – the name which appears next to the picture of the girl in the locket.

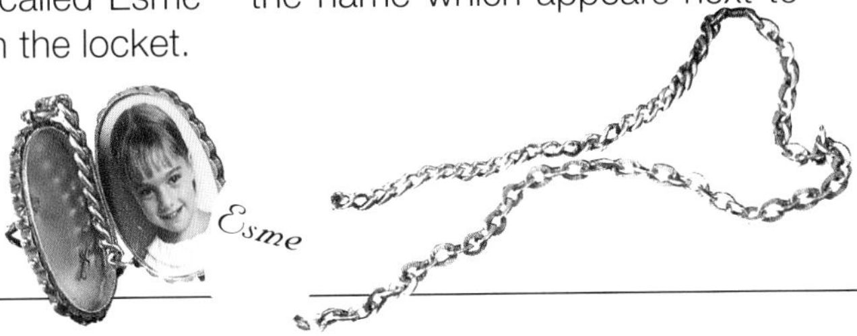
Esme

Pages 124 & 125

The sailing cap dropped on the ground looks remarkably like the one worn by Kurt McBurns on the front of his leaflet about '*The Kurt McBurns Wonderful World of Piratical Plunder and Loot*' pirate theme park, on page 119.

There is also a business card with the initials *K.M.W.W.P.P.L.* printed on it – the initials Kurt uses as a shortened version of his theme park in a newspaper article on page 115.

Sticking out of a basket of fruit is the corner of a box with a very familiar pattern on it. It looks identical to the illegal box of fondant creams that was half-hidden on Dr. Greygoose's desk on page 117.

Pages 126 & 127

In Jane Anchorage's article on page 115, Septimus Splicer is quoted as saying: 'I'm a magician and I never go anywhere without my pot of vanishing powder.'

There is a pot of vanishing powder on the bed!

Pages 128 & 129

In a newspaper article on page 115, it is stated that Lil is 'a diver for the Espinola Maritime Museum' – the organization you're working for under Dr. Greygoose. It also states that she 'holds the Pearl Diver Association's coveted *Golden Clothespeg Award* for holding her breath underwater for six minutes'.

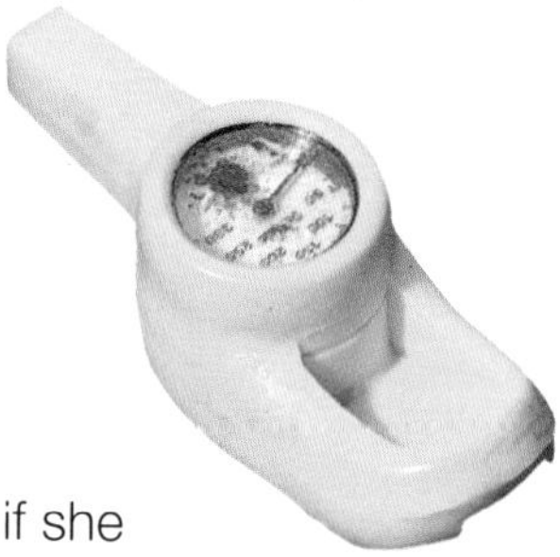

This suggests that Lil Monkey would be in the least trouble if she went diving without oxygen.

Pages 130 & 131

The plunger has 'PROPERTY OF C.COLLINS' written on it (in long-lasting waterproof ink!). In the *Disgraceful*'s dutybook, which appears on page 100, the name '*Crowsnest Collins*' appears under 11:30am cannon painting – fortunately, the book was saved according to the clipping entitled '**Pirate's possessions presented to pub**' on page 114.

C. COLLINS could very possibly be Crowsnest Collins, so these items *are* likely to be from the wreck of the sunken *Disgraceful*.

Pages 132 & 133

There are, in fact, three coded messages waiting for you in the Radio Room. Two can be deciphered using the Morse Code keys pinned to the wall.

Once decoded, the first of these, **MORSE CODE MESSAGE NO. 1**, is the question 'WHAT GOES ZZUB ZZUB' and the second, **MORSE CODE MESSAGE NO. 2**, is the answer 'A BEE REVERSING'. They must be some kind of a joke!

The third message is in the form of three flags on the desk. Once decoded using the key pinned to the wall in the top left-hand corner, they read: BEWARE PIRATES ON BOARD. But there is nothing to suggest who the warning is from.

Pages 134 & 135

The note is, in fact, in a very simple code. The words are in the same order that they would be in an ordinary message – it's just that the order of the *letters* in each word have been reversed. Decoded, the message reads:

GONE TO DIG UP TREASURE ON ISLAND
LIL, SEPTIMUS AND KURT
P.S. HOPE YOU LIKED OUR MESSAGES IN THE RADIO ROOM

They have probably gone in search of the treasure on Saffron Island because, according to Captain Blackeye's logbook entry on page 127, Incense Island and Cardamon Island are both completely surrounded by dangerous rocks and '*only Saffron Island will be approachable by boat*'. This must be where the original Monkey, McBurns and Splicer buried the casket of doubloons over two hundred years ago.

Pages 136 & 137

To be able to answer the question *'Where is King Oswald's treasure?'* you must first be sure *what* it is. Blackeye's latest note suggests that the doubloons aren't his real treasure . . . but are there any clues earlier in the adventure that might back up this statement? Try looking at pages 130 & 131 again.

Once you think you know where King Oswald of Espinola's stolen treasure is hidden, then – and only then – turn the page and hold the solution up to a mirror . . .

THE SOLUTION

King Oswald's stolen treasure is certainly not in the possession of Lil Monkey, Kurt McBurns or Septimus Splicer. The gold doubloons in the small casket they dug up on Saffron Island were never a part of King Oswald's treasure. Blackeye wasn't lying when he referred to them in his note on page 136 as 'fool's gold'.

In your orders on page 99, Admiral Bandybow of the Espinolan Navy says that every piece of gold from King Oswald's stolen treasure '*is marked with our National emblem*'. These doubloons are, however, marked with a special cross – similar to one that appears on a bottle of grog on page 130. The grog is '**Made in Rustica**' and '**Bears Rustican national emblem**'. You can see from the chart, on page 103, that Rustica is a separate country from Espinola. Therefore, since the doubloons carry the Rustican emblem, they can't be King Oswald's treasure.

So where is the real treasure? Captain Blackeye left plenty of clues. Once decoded, the message on page 120 says '*Look for the maiden with golden hair*'. The only girls with golden hair are Esme, Blackeye's daughter, whose picture appears in the locket on page 122, and the figurehead which used to be on the front of Blackeye's ship, the Disgraceful. According to the advertisement on page 118, the Captain's little daughter Esme was the model for the figurehead.

In his entry in the logbook shown on page 127, Blackeye states that he '*left behind Disgraceful's figurehead for repainting at Espinola Port*'. He then writes about testing '*Gold-i-lux*' paint. In the duty book on page 100, two pirates are listed to '*paint cannons red and yellow using special paint*'. A red and yellow tin of '*Gold-i-lux*' paint appear on the deck on page 111. In an advertisement on page 119 '*Gold-i-lux*' is described as being specially formulated '**to cover 24 carat gold**'. . . So, according to the logbook, the figurehead of Blackeye's ship has been removed and is being painted with a special paint designed to cover gold.

On page 114, the article about Captain Blackeye in the book says: '**Another theory is that King Oswald's treasure was melted down, made into one large object and painted over to disguise its true identity**'. This theory was correct.

Captain Blackeye removed the figurehead from his ship, had King Oswald's treasure melted down and shaped like the missing figurehead – then had it painted to look like the original. Because he was captured, the pirate captain could never retrieve the golden figurehead. And where is it now? As the advertisement says on page 118, the figurehead is on show at Espinola City Port. . . King Oswald's treasure has been right under everyone's nose all the time!

First published in 1995 by Usborne Publishing Limited, Usborne House, 83-85 Saffron Hill, London EC1N 8RT, England.

Printed in Spain U.E. First published in America March 1996